THROUGH THE STORM

Sydnee's Showers of Blessings and Lessons

RENE MERRITT

Self -n- DAYS
Publish 30

This Is The Year for
Your New Book

WWW.SELFPUBLISHN30DAYS.COM

Printed in the United States of America

ISBN: 978-1688757332

1. Fiction 2. Inspiration
Rene Merritt.
Through the Storm

DEDICATION

To my wonderful parents, Ben and Shirley Wolfe, thank you for always encouraging and supporting me wholeheartedly through every season of my life. I appreciate your unconditional love, your advice and your prayers. I will forever be grateful for your wisdom, guidance and patience. I'm very thankful for the vital role you played in helping me raise my kids to be the successful and respectful young adults they are today.

You both mean so much more to me than words can begin to express. I appreciate you and I love you with all that I am.

To my kiddos, Trene' and Trevor Merritt and Camron Chaney: Our love is undeniable and unexplainable. Our relationship is genuine and our bond is unbreakable. I love you guys with every fiber of my being. Thank you for your unconditional love, support and encouragement. I am truly blessed to be your mother. I thank you for your patience, because things weren't always easy, but our struggle strengthened me. Our bad days made me appreciate the good. Because of you, I'm always striving to be and do better.

Just know this is only the beginning and the best is yet to come. As I always say, "I grind, you grind, we eat together."

In loving memory of my best friend, Jackie Lyons (1976–2007)

In loving memory of my father, Choice Booth (1957–2014)

In loving memory of my godson, LaDarius Bentley (1996–2017)

ACKNOWLEDGMENTS

Through my pain, I've found my purpose. Through my weakness, I've learned to depend on God's strength. I've turned my wounds into wisdom, and my pain into power.

I am humbled, thankful and blessed that in such a graceful and merciful way, God showed me that without him, I am nothing.

To my Smith family, in particular, my Grandmother Eva, "Ma-Ma," and my uncle Gene, thank you for being such an active part of my upbringing. It truly takes a village and I appreciate the way you supported my mother in raising me. Thank you for supporting my dreams throughout the years. Thank you for the knowledge and love you poured into me and for the knowledge and love you continue to pour into my children.

My cousin Nick, you are just as quiet, observant and supportive as your dad, and I thank you from the bottom of my heart for everything. I love you like a brother.

To one of my besties, Tiffaney Ross, we met in Gulfport, Mississippi when

Cash Money Records was taking over in 1999. We were two very young military wives, away from home, away from our families, and most of the time, away from our husbands, but we had each other. Neither distance nor years will ever lessen the love I have for you. Thank you for keeping my secrets, thank you for your friendship, thank you for your brutal honesty. Thank you for being sincere. Most of all, thank you for being you and for accepting me for who I am.

To my other bestie, Alfreda Watkins, and my good friend, Michelle Hardwick. You two ladies have supported me and encouraged me through some of the toughest times of my life. You supported me throughout the entire process of writing this book. You motivated me, inspired me, and spoke life into me on the days when I wanted to quit. I'm glad you saw my potential and recognized my worth when I didn't. While others walked away, you embraced my growth. You pushed me to do and be better. I'm thankful for the genuineness of our friendship. I thank you for your loyalty and your honesty. I thank you for being exactly who you are, and for allowing me to be exactly who I am. I'm blessed to have you both in my life. I love you.

To my church family at Bethel SDA Church, with special mention of the Jones, Reeves, and Thomas/Shepherd families, I thank you for your prayers, love and support, not only for me, but for my children as well. Toni, thanks for always reminding me to pay my tithes. We are blessed to belong to such a caring, loving spiritual family.

It's hard to believe that I've worked with some of the same people since 2005. To my coworkers at CMS and ES who've become more like family, I thank you for the laughs and the friendships.

I remember saying how we've watched each other's kids grow up, but honestly, we've also watched each other grow, mature and evolve. We've shared weddings, baby showers and funerals together. I thank you for the encouragement, support, and love over the last 14 years.

I especially want to thank Katia Behrmann, who I worked closely with the last several years. You probably know more about me than my closest friends. You've been there through it all. Sometimes, not by choice, but you never complained. You've been there through many of my storms, and not once did you judge me. I'm so grateful for your honesty, compassion, and understanding. Thank you for sharing your wisdom and knowledge with me. Most of all, thank you for your patience and prayers.

Even as adults, it takes a village and I'm so grateful for mine. Thanks to those who never doubted me, nor gave up on me. Thank you for taking the time to get to know me and for understanding who I am. Thank you for giving me the time and space to grow, and for loving me as I did so.

Lastly, to Darren Palmer and his awesome staff at Self Publish -N- 30 Days, YOU ROCK! Thanks for your patience and for believing in me. Because of you, my dream has become reality.

Many Blessings,
Rene Merritt

TABLE OF CONTENTS

INTRODUCTION

"I've gone through the fire
And I've been through the flood.
I've been broken into pieces,
Seen lightning flash from above.
But through it all, I remember
That He loves me
And He cares
And He'll never put more on me
Than I can bear."

"MORE THAN I CAN BEAR"
BY KIRK FRANKLIN & GOD'S PROPERTY

Hey guys! Allow me to introduce myself. I'm Sydnee McCullen, a 42-year-old single mother of four beautiful children. I had my first two children at the age of 16; twin girls, Teigan and Raigan. They are both college graduates and married. They have moved away from home, but thankfully, are only a few hours away.

Two years after the twins were born, my third child, Keegan, was born. He is a senior in college and plays basketball and I'm grateful he is only a couple of hours away from home.

Klyde is the youngest and came along when I was 20 years old. Although Klyde is the baby of the bunch, he is the most independent and furthest away from home. He's in his sophomore year in college.

Growing up, I had 'statistic' written all over me. I was raised by a single mother, and there I was, repeating the cycle, but I was determined to be the successful young lady that my mom taught me to be.

I did a few things backwards, but how rewarding it is to defy all odds. I graduated from high school, then went onto college and I raised four successful kids with the help of my mom and stepdad, who came into our lives when I was 17.

At the age of 39, I was just starting to embrace my empty nest and enjoy my newfound freedom. I enrolled back in school just to take some business classes. I had recently received a promotion on my job. The promotion came with more money, but also with a lot more responsibilities.

I started travelling with The Grown and Sexy group and quickly realized, it was more than just a travel group, it's a big family. We laugh and cry together. We support and encourage each other. We even had people who've donated their kidney to other members of the group.

We had just returned from Costa Rica and were heading to Aruba next. I was booked with a few friends and was looking forward to the vacation.

Everything was falling into place. I was enjoying the fruits of my labor. I was at a place of fulfillment and peace. I'd never been married, and after a few failed relationships, I was even interested in dating again. That is, until unhealed wounds started to bleed on my new relationship.

As I share my story, my opinions, my deepest thoughts and my experiences, my lessons and blessings, it will give you a peek into some real issues women face today. It will touch on things we may be too embarrassed to share, thinking that we are alone and that no one will relate or that no one will understand. We may think no one cares or that people will judge, ridicule or shame us. My story touches on faith, spirituality, social media, mental illness, healing, the importance of being transparent and the importance of supportive, praying family and friends.

Some women were taught that when life comes at you hard and fast, that we are to just hush, be strong and take it, but we do get tired and weak at times. We get so caught up being everything to everybody else and we tend to forget about ourselves.

As you read this, you may want to fasten your seatbelts, because this will be a bumpy ride as I take you into my mind, to my emotions, through my heart, and right into my soul.

"If you don't mind, can I be far from perfect?
Just can I be me?
Do you have time to see?
What a work in progress reeled in me
Spent many nights on my knees,
'Cause that's the key for me to be free.
A thousand tears, a million goals
Just some ingredients that helped me to grow.
Got to pay, added some sun and rain.
Blended it together with grace.
But still I had to wait,
'Cause he wanted me to be strong
For the days I know are long

RENE MERRITT

And all of my superpowers were gone.
He said I'm making something better, I'm
putting it all together.
Trust me."

"IF YOU DON'T MIND"

BY LEDISI & KIRK FRANKLIN

CHAPTER 1
PERFECT TIMING

Ring, ring, ring. I pulled my desk drawer opened and grabbed my cell phone to see who was calling me. I was a little curious because it was an unfamiliar number but since it was a local number, I answered.

"Hello?"

The deep, sexy voice on the other end replied, "Hey you."

The voice sounded a little familiar, and even though I was unsure, I replied back, "Hey, how are you?"

And he replied, "I'm better now that I'm talking to you!"

Wait, this can't be! "Is this Storm?!"

He gave a cute little chuckle as he replied, "Yes!"

Oh, my goodness, after all this time he still has my number.

Wow, it was a blast from my past, Ian Crawford. Ian stood about 5'8" and had a small build, but was muscular, strong and powerful, earning the nickname Storm from his teammates while on the wrestling team in high school. The name stuck with him throughout his time in the military, through college and right into his adulthood.

I got up from my desk to walk outside to finish our conversation, because I knew it was about to get juicy.

Storm and I met about six years prior. He had just gone through his third divorce and I was dealing with a recent break up. We were introduced by a mutual friend who thought we could both use a friend.

Storm and I hit it off. We started spending a lot of time together and even though we both agreed we weren't ready for a serious relationship, I could tell that feelings were brewing. When things would start to heat up and get serious between us, Storm would put up a little resistance and we'd slow down. But it was happening so naturally, that soon enough we were back at a place where Storm was more afraid to go than I was. We went through a rash of emotions. There were a lot of ups and downs and on and offs for about two years before mutually falling away from each other and eventually becoming just friends. We stayed in touch until Storm took a teaching job out of state. I was almost glad that he left, because I needed the distance. I needed to clear my head.

But now Storm was back.

As I walked back inside the office, my coworker, Katie, who was my mom's age, and just as observant as she was happy, spun around in her chair looking at me. I tried not to smile, but dark as I am, I'm sure my face was red.

I looked at her and asked, "What?!"

"Well, Sydnee, who was that?" she asked.

I really started blushing. "That was Storm. He and I used to date a while back," I replied.

Katie just smiled and turned back to her desk. Lord, I couldn't hold it in.

I blurted out, "Girl, he's interested in us dating again but this time he wants something more serious."

"And what are you going to do, Sydnee?" she asked.

I replied, "I'm not really sure, Katie. He's a really good person and I care about him a lot, but the first time we dated was such an emotional roller coaster ride, but maybe that's because we were both fresh out of bad relationships." Katie agreed and as always told me to pray about it and not to rush into anything. I just replied, "I know," as her words went in one ear and out the other.

The workday ended, and I could not wait to get home and call Storm back. That night we talked for almost two hours. We were just catching up on each other's lives, reminiscing about the past and talking about the future. It was such an awkward conversation to be having with Storm, because during our first relationship, we really didn't share our feelings. Well, I did, but Storm hid his.

For the most part, Storm had kept up with me via social media, but I had no idea. He was the social media junkie who'd scroll and look, but would rarely post or comment. I almost forgot we were friends on social media until he started talking about my recent trips. He was amazed at how grown up my kids were. He said he was proud of me for mentoring. He mentioned my weight loss, and spoke highly of a red dress I had recently worn to a party. Storm had done his homework.

The next day, we texted and talked throughout the workday. Again, that night we spent almost two hours on the phone. We just laughed and talked like two teenagers, all bubbly and giddy inside.

Storm was wanting to take me to dinner that upcoming weekend, but I already had plans with Teigan and Raigan on Friday. Then, on Saturday I had plans with the girls.

Oh shit, the girls! OH, MY GOODNESS, wait until I tell the girls who I'm talking to again!

See, my girls mean everything to me. We've been through so much together and I love them like sisters. We respect each other's opinions and choices, but I was sure they'd have a lot to say about Storm.

At dinner on Saturday night, I filled the girls in on my news about Storm.

The girls consisted of Maya, who was divorced, but had recently started dating; Kimber, who was single but mingling; Frankie was engaged and just like, Stephanie, she still had minor children at home; and although Stephanie had gotten married and moved away, she was still very much a part of my immediate circle. She would have to be caught up on the news later.

Maya and Frankie were both very excited for me. They both thought the time and distance between Storm and me gave us both a chance to grow. They believed he was sincere and they were hopeful that things would work out for him and me this time. They both told me to just guard my heart, and like Katie, they wanted me to take it slow.

Kimber was happy as well, but showed a little concern for my feelings. That was understandable, because she was the one I confided in the most during my first relationship with Storm. She knew a lot more than the other girls. She knew how hard I had fallen for him.

I then teased the girls that Storm had been cyberstalking me. They laughed and said, "Well, at least he knows what he's getting into!"

Later that night after dinner, I spoke to Stephanie. Stephanie is the youngest and most outspoken one of the group. That girl is so blunt you can smoke her and I love it. I still laugh at our conversation.

"Hey Steph, how are you?"

"Hey Syd, I'm good. How are you?"

"Girl, I'm good. Guess who called me Monday?!"

"Tre? Mike? Derrick?"

THROUGH THE STORM

After a few wrong guesses, I laughed and said, "No, girl! Storm called!"

After a slight pause, she yelled, "And what did his raggedy ass want?!" Lord, I was skeptical about telling her *everything*, but I decided to continue, and I knew I had to quickly defend Storm in order for her to even calm down enough to hear me out!

I told her that Storm was back in town and we'd started talking. Again I continued saying Storm was different and just in the last few days he'd been trying to show me that more than ever he's willing to try. No one is perfect, so effort was all I needed. I even told her that Maya and Frankie both agreed that Storm and I both had time to grow and think about the things that transpired between us previously. Storm had definitely led me to believe he had changed and he was well aware that I had too.

Stephanie chuckled as she reminded me that once Storm and I ended our first relationship, I was so mentally exhausted that it took me two years to get myself together. I laughed because it was partly true. Actually, it was all true. I did need time to reset. I spent a full two years single. Yes, "single, single." I mean no booty calls, no dating, no fly-by-nights, no sex, no friends with benefits! NOTHING. I had been totally focused on myself and on raising my children. In my opinion, I did a great job. During that time, I even learned to let go of Keegan and Klyde's father, with his tall, dark and handsome self. I had allowed him all access to me when he came to visit the boys, which honestly, wasn't often enough.

Before Stephanie and I got off the phone, she accepted the idea that maybe Storm was serious and sincere this time. Thankfully, she gave me her blessings and wished me well.

A week later, Storm and I finally went on our highly anticipated date. We met for dinner, drinks and adult conversation. It had been over a year since I'd been on a date. As a matter of fact, I had only dated one other guy

9

since my last relationship with Storm. Don't get me wrong though, I'm not saying I didn't have a reliable friend to rendezvous with when I needed to.

The date went very well, but I expected nothing less. Storm and I had such a connection. Everything flowed so naturally that we were already making plans for our second date, which was the very next night. Storm was interested in hearing one of his favorite bands that was playing at a local venue. The idea of live music, food, drinks and good company sounded perfect to me, so I decided to go with him. I hadn't dressed up in a while, and I had the perfect dress.

Storm was excited that I agreed to accompany him. He mentioned that he wanted me to meet one of his old friends that was a member of the band. I was thinking, *He's wanting me to meet people already?* I wasn't sure how to feel about that, but I knew it was important to him, so I obliged. See, since moving back, Storm had started practicing and doing guest appearances with his old band. He was so damn talented and diverse.

Storm had retired from teaching, but would work per diem as a substitute teacher, which wasn't often. His biggest accomplishment was starting and running his own business. Storm had opened a men's clothing store. That was so perfect for him, because he was well-known for his sense of fashion and style. He was always well groomed and dressed nicely. Did I mention he always smelled so good and was dark, handsome and charming? My God, it felt like I hit the lotto. Old as I am and single as I was, I had no business having a type, but if I did, Storm was it.

The second date went great as well. We laughed, talked, sang and danced. It had been a while since I'd slow danced, and it felt so good to be pressed up against Storm's buff chest. I could feel his peppermint breath on my neck as he pulled me closer and held me tighter. Storm was so strong, yet very gentle.

THROUGH THE STORM

That night was the first time I saw Storm's goofy and silly side when he pulled out his cell phone and we began taking silly selfies. He never posted the pictures or shared them with anyone that I know of, and I almost forgot we had taken the pictures until he sent them to me in a collage for our one-month anniversary.

After the band performance, we went back to Storm's house. The vibe was amazing. We just sat in his car in the driveway for hours. We talked about us and where we wanted to go from there. We were both at a different place in our lives, a much better place than a few years ago.

Storm apologized about the way things ended with us previously and vowed to give it his all this time. He told me that he had been wanting to reach out to me for a while, but was afraid of rejection. He told me that once he prayed about it, he felt comfortable enough to do so. *Wow, he prayed for me? He prayed about us? He has changed!*

After listening to him and hearing him out, I accepted what he was saying as the truth. If I had changed, who was I to say that he hadn't? Besides, he had no reason to lie to me, right?

We both agreed that this was the perfect time to start over. We wanted to try this relationship thing again. I know I was good and ready.

We then shared a kiss so passionate and powerful that all the feelings I had buried for Storm came rushing back. *My God!!* And, it didn't help that he whispered in my ear, "Damn Syd, you just don't know how much I've missed you!" I really missed him, too. I missed his touch, his passion, his smell, his smile, damn. But most of all, I missed us ordering pizza late at night and watching back-to-back episodes of Mary Mary.

Storm then invited me in, and even though I was tempted, I resisted the offer. Instead, I got out of his car and right into mine, but not before Storm smacked me on the butt and kissed me, again. I almost changed my mind about leaving, but I went on home with a big smile on my face.

When I got to work the next day, I dropped an anonymous message in our "happy jar." It read "I went on a date this weekend, it went very well and I'm excited to see where things go from here." At the beginning of the year, we decided we needed to boost the moral at work year round. The happy jar was implemented so we could drop in encouraging notes, positive quotes and any good or exciting news we wanted to share. At quarterly staff meetings, we would pick notes from the jar and read them out loud. We were hoping that on our bad days, these would remind us of the good ones.

Two months passed and Storm and I were dating exclusively. After about three weeks, I had pretty much moved in. I was staying at his place at least five days a week. When I would crank up my car, even the GPS on my smartphone knew exactly where I was headed. It's said it takes twenty-one days to form a habit and Storm had quickly become an important part of my life.

Everything seemed so perfect. Even though we dated before, we shared so many "firsts."

I met one of his sons and he met my four kids. We were cooking dinner together. We were double dating with his friends and their significant others. We were going to concerts, comedy shows and sporting events together. Storm told me that we had more in those two months than he had done in about two years. He was finally enjoying life, and we were glad to be back apart of each others' lives. All of the feelings and love that Storm held back during our first relationship was now pouring out of him.

Things were moving so fast that it started to frighten me a little, but the girls always told me to stop worrying and reminded me to just breathe.

THROUGH THE STORM

They asked, "Isn't this what both of you wanted?" "Isn't this what you guys talked about, Syd?" *Yes, I guess it was.* Storm was proving himself to me. Storm was showing me the man he had grown to be. Storm and I were both tired of the games, secrets, uncertainties and failed relationships. We were committed to making things work this time. Besides, we were two adults who were already well acquainted with each other, so why put a timeframe on falling in love?

Maya was the praying friend, and like my coworker Katie, they both kept telling me to "just pray about it" and I wanted this to work so bad that I did. I prayed for my man. I prayed for our relationship. I think that was probably the first time I sincerely prayed about a relationship. I was serious about Storm.

It was now a week before Storm's 49th birthday, and he was dropping cute little hints about what he wanted to do. Me, always being so attentive to him, quickly started planning. I did get his input on a few things, because I wanted this to be perfect. A few days before his birthday, the plans were final.

The day before his birthday, I told him our plans, because we needed to start packing and hit the road. Storm would wake up in Savannah, Georgia on his special day. Savannah is such a beautiful city. It's so romantic, and to me, it's a couple's city. That was the perfect place for a weekend getaway. I was also excited, because that was the first time Storm and I had been out of town together. We enjoyed every minute of it. We soaked it all in. The peace and quiet, the long talks, the late night walks, the romantic dinners and the hot and heated love making—on the balcony, in the bed, in the shower—my goodness. Just like a good wine, the sex had gotten better over time.

I had thought of everything I could to make this a memorable weekend for Storm, except for one thing. I had forgotten to get him a birthday cake. I mean, what's a birthday without cake? Thank God for google and GPS, because I found a bakery and got him a vanilla cake, just like he wanted. Even though I teased him that I was all the sweetness he needed.

Later that night, I heard Storm on the phone with one of his good friends telling him that this was one of the best birthdays he'd had. He was describing the hotel room and the breathtaking view; he was talking about how great dinner was. He was so happy and appreciative. I just smiled. Thankfully, I nailed it, and to me, my baby deserved it. We had such a good time; I was already thinking about Jamaica for his 50th.

It was almost hard to believe the complete turnaround Storm had made. At this point, only a few people knew we were dating. We weren't hiding it, but we weren't broadcasting it either.

I remember telling the girls how different Storm was and how much he had changed. Things were so different compared to the first time we dated. Everyone was so happy for us, especially Maya, who often said, "You deserve it, Syd, this is your time!" *Yesssss, it was my time.* I was so happy. I was glowing. I had love written all over me! I finally decided to let my wall down. I decided to just go with the flow, and boy, was it flowing fast! Storm had me going. My heart was jumping and my head was spinning, just like the big wheels on his truck.

A couple of weeks after returning from Savannah, things got a little more serious between Storm and I. He met my parents and I met his. That was such a big deal to me, mainly because I'm very family-oriented and I wanted him to be part of that. I wanted him to get to know my family. I wanted him to be a part of our Sunday dinners and our Saturday game nights. Also, in the two years we dated previously, us meeting each other's parents was never a thought, and he made sure I knew I was the first woman he had "taken home to momma" in a long time.

A few days later, Storm started asking questions that shocked me. He wanted to know my ring size. Storm started hinting that Savannah would be the perfect place for "someone" to propose, and said his next tattoo would be my initials on his ring finger. He started ending his text messages to me with #TeamCrawford. He wanted to know when my lease was up on my apartment. He was asking if he needed to change the décor in his home. It was definitely a bachelor's pad, but I had no complaints. He had such great taste. We were even planning vacations together. *Whooaaaa, what in the hell was happening?* I just kept thinking, *Wow, Storm is a different man. He has really changed.* He was all in and I liked it.

A few minutes after I would leave for work in the mornings, Storm would text me that he missed me already. That text would be followed by another text telling me how aroused he was because he could still smell the scent of my perfume in the room. Storm sure knew how to keep me smiling throughout the day.

Storm started consulting me about clothing ideas for his store, and about music and venue options for his band. I felt fully included in his life.

We even made a trip back to Savannah just to visit "Better Than Sex," an upscale romantic restaurant that serves only decadent desserts, but there was nothing better than the dessert I gave him later that night.

As we sat in a restaurant one afternoon, he even suggested we make our first post together on social media. I was skeptical, but I agreed. It wasn't even a picture of us, but of our champagne glasses, because that day, we were truly celebrating us. We made a commitment to each other. Once we posted, we laughed and said, "Now, we're official."

I know people love to say when you should or shouldn't tell people about your relationship or when you should or shouldn't post on social media, but I see it like this, social media doesn't ruin relationships, people do. Social media may expose a weak relationship, but it's up to the two individuals to make it work. You can be in a serious relationship for years and it still not be solid. You can be married for years with kids, and it still not be solid. A relationship is going to be what it's going to be, depending on the couple. It will last or it's going to crumble, on or off of social media.

Besides, who wants to be in a relationship that you have to hide? Who wants to sneak around? Who wants to be with someone who isn't proud to have them or scared to admit openly that they love or care about them? I sure don't. I want to be excited about love, not holding back with the fear of being embarrassed or with the fear that the relationship may fail. We should be able to love loud and love free.

CHAPTER 2
CLOUDY WITH A
CHANCE OF PAIN

"Sometimes I think pain is just a lack of understanding.
If we could only understand it all, would we feel no pain?
God must feel no pain, only joy
Does this mean even our suffering pleases him?"

"ONCE AN ADDICT" BY J. COLE

Shortly after becoming "official," basketball season had started back for Keegan and I was constantly on the go, but so was Storm, who was now in full swing with his band, and his business was booming.

As with anything important to me, I made time to support Storm in every aspect of his life. In between my job and being the unofficial team mom for Keegan, I was going to his shows, running errands for his business and making sure he was good at home also. Being a single mother of four kids for so long prepared me for this. I was used to being all over the place, and honestly, I missed it. I missed feeling needed.

Even on my most hectic days, I never uttered a complaint, so it surprised me when Storm started asking, "Are you ready for this, are you sure you're built for this?"

"Yes, I am!" I said.

"Are you sure? Because it's about to get hectic and chaotic," he replied.

I said, "I live for hectic and chaotic. Let's do this!"

Then he jokingly said, "You know music will always be my wife, and you'll always be my mistress." I laughed it off, but something was telling me that he was dead ass serious. I was now thinking, *Hell, is he ready for this?* Storm must have thought he was dealing with the old Sydnee, but the new one was nobody's damn mistress.

We were almost four months into our relationship, and my trip to Aruba was quickly approaching, and it couldn't have been more at the wrong time. Storm was now depending on me a lot, both mentally and physically, and Keegan was struggling with his grades and that was affecting his performance on the court. Honestly, if the trip had not already been booked and paid for, I would not have gone. I was having anxiety about the flight. Storm was having anxiety about the duration of my trip. The next couple of weeks would be hell.

I started to sense a little resentment from Storm. Perhaps he was feeling unsure and uneasy, but there was no way he didn't trust me. I just couldn't put my finger on it. At no point had I given him a reason to doubt me, but I do know he was so adamant about getting things right with our relationship this time around that he started reading my horoscope. Instead of the results of the horoscope reading being encouraging to him, I think it did the opposite. He was intimidated when he read that the Sagittarius woman is independent and loves her freedom. That was true about me, but I loved him more, and I knew I could still be independent while in a relationship. I could be strong and fierce, yet submissive. I had already proven that to him.

Nonetheless, the questions started, and most of them were about the men in the travel group. I was confused. If I wanted to hook up with someone, I wouldn't have to go all the way to Aruba. I wanted to say, "Do you know how many local dudes are in my inbox?" Instead, I just reassured him that everything between us was great. I explained to him that even when I was single, I travelled to explore the world, not to hook up. I had no reason to mess around on him. I made sure he knew that I would never risk our relationship for a few days of fun. Besides, did he forget I went a full two years without a man and without sex? I can surely go eight days with no problem. I may catch other guys' attention, but I only wanted his. Storm had my heart.

The day before my trip, I was quite busy doing last minute shopping and getting my hair braided up. Storm and I both got home late that night. I walked in and he had just gotten home also. He looked at my hair and said, "It's cute, but you know I like it long." Before I could say anything, I looked over and saw a dozen roses on the night stand near my side of the bed. Storm had surprised me with flowers. I was so happy, but mostly, relieved.

That night we made love like it was our last time. Afterwards, his hands were shaking and he could barely hold the bottle of water we both desperately needed. It was hot as hell and my hair was wet. I remember being thankful his son wasn't home. Because for one, the moans were fierce and the banging of the headboard was so loud, he would've heard us, and two, I wasn't about to put on any clothes as I went to adjust the A/C. Later, as Storm held me, I could still feel his body trembling. I looked up at him and smiled, he smiled back, and with tears in his big, round, hazel eyes, he told me I was the best thing that had happened to him.

He was going to be just fine while I was gone, after all... So I thought.

The next morning, Storm woke up in a bad mood. He, all of a sudden, wasn't feeling well and said he couldn't take me to the airport. At my age, my parents still rescue me. That morning, my stepdad dropped what he was doing and came right over to take me to the airport. Storm was still lying in bed when my stepdad rang the doorbell. I asked Storm if was he going to walk me outside, but he just rolled over.

Also, during the trip, Storm became very distant as he had during most of my trips to Keegan's away basketball games. This time it was very noticeable. The cute little text messages stopped. He used to text me the lyrics of "Boo'd Up" by Ella Mai and "Giving You the Best That I Got" by Anita Baker, but his favorite was "Sydnee, do you love me? Are you riding? Say you'll never ever leave from beside me," and I'd reply back, "Because I want you and I need you." Yep, Drake's song "In My Feelings" was our anthem!

While I was gone, if I called or texted him, the conversation was short. The hashtag was no longer at the end of his text messages.

Was he mad? Was he jealous? Nah, he knows I love him and he knows I'm all in. Was he trying to ruin my trip?

I just couldn't figure out why he was feeling so insecure and being so cold. Although I enjoyed my trip for the most part, not knowing what to expect when I got home created a dark cloud over me, and I know my roommate felt the effects.

Upon my return home, Storm did at least pick me up from the airport. I was happy to see him. As a matter of fact, while everyone else received t-shirts, magnets and key chains as gifts, I had gotten Storm a small bottle of one of his favorite colognes. I remember teasing him saying that he had to be my husband first before he earned the next size. Despite his actions while I was away, I missed him. I spent the day at my mom's house because Keegan and Klyde were in town for a short visit, but I ended the night with Storm.

THROUGH THE STORM

Over the next few days, I started to notice a change in Storm. He was becoming so defensive and sensitive about every, and any, little thing. He was moody. Our normal routine started to be a problem for him. For example, by him running his own business, he had the freedom to talk or text during the workday, unlike me. On my breaks or during lunch is when I would have the time to chat and I would reach out then. When I would ask Storm, "Hey babe, what are you up to?" his replies went from, "Just thinking about you" to "What am I supposed to be up to?" It was like he was guilty or something.

Our biggest issues came when Storm started complaining about my social media. He and I had been followers of each other for years now. As a matter of fact, we were followers before we started dating, so nothing I posted should've been surprising to him. It was nothing different than before and it definitely wasn't anything offensive toward him, but Storm insisted that people were coming in the store asking about my page and about my post. He said people were calling him asking him about the memes I was sharing. *Like, really?! Memes? Doesn't everyone share memes?*

My only defense was, "Well, Storm you have access to my page. What do *YOU* think my post meant?" My next question was, "Who are these people and why do they even feel comfortable enough coming to you about me anyways?" Apparently, Storm's loyalty was with "these people," because he would never tell me who was saying these things. I just wanted to delete the troublemakers, but he just boldly replied, "I never delete my enemies from my social media, I like for them to see what I'm doing." *What? Enemies? I have enemies, now?* I just wanted some peace and quiet in my household. Was that too much to ask?

Those rough days turned into rough weeks, and things were hectic and chaotic just as Storm had predicted. It didn't help that Storm had been having headaches and dealing with sinus issues. Understandably, that combination had him very irritable and moody, but this started to remind me of the old Storm, always frustrated, stressed and indecisive about everything. I was starting to wonder if Storm had really changed.

Even questions like what he wanted for dinner became hard to answer. His appetite was changing. His blood pressure was up, and I had to start reminding him to take his medication.

Storm also had issues with a close friend who was actually one of his store employees. He was giving Storm a hard time about his pay, and about Storm being away from the store so much. The employee felt he deserved a raise, and although Storm had started depending on him a lot more, he disagreed.

Storm was now doing two shows a week. It seemed like he was working at the store, practicing for a show, or doing a show. He was putting in 10-hour days, six days a week. I was still working full-time, and my new position produced many challenges. I would still try to mentor every now and again, support Storm and Keegan, and squeeze in a social life.

By the end of most nights, Storm and I were both so tired that once we were home, we would just eat and crash. When the nights out and sex slowed up, it really didn't bother me, because we both needed the rest, especially Storm, who had started becoming very anxious and restless during the night.

Five months into the relationship, and three months after Storm's birthday, my fortieth birthday was approaching. I was so excited. I've always made my birthdays and the kid's birthdays a big deal. I almost lost my life when I gave birth to the twins, and I almost lost them as well. Just to be alive was a blessing and we always celebrate big. I was ready to embrace the big 4-0! I had special dinner plans with my family and close friends and this year, I would have my new man by my side. I was rolling up on forty in style and was thinking that this was going to be huge.

The weekend before my birthday, as tradition, the girls planned to take me out. A couple of days before going, the girls and I talked and thought maybe we should ask the guys to join us and make it a couple's night instead. It had been a while since all of us were romantically involved with someone at the same time.

I knew Storm's schedule was tight, and I was just appreciative that he was able to clear his busy schedule and was going to be at my dinner the following weekend, but I asked anyways. Storm reminded me that he had to work late and try to get in a quick practice after work. I was fine with that, especially knowing that next weekend specifically belonged to me. Plus, that actually gave me time to catch up with my girls. I was missing them! Although my relationship with Storm was top priority, I didn't want the girls to think I had forgotten about them.

As I got dressed to go out, "aunt flow" came to visit. Yep, my cycle started a few days early. As I went from wearing a light colored, fitted dress to some black leather leggings, I laughed. That explained why I had been craving pasta and over analyzing everything.

As I was leaving the house, Storm was pulling up. I quickly kissed him, but was careful not to smear my lipstick and I hopped in the car. It was a Friday night and I was on my merry way with my girls and we were about to turn up!

We had a really good time, as usual. I love to dance, so we danced all night! We took pictures, Kimber was going "live." It was a night to remember. I enjoyed the girls a lot, but I was equally glad for the night to be coming to an end. I was tired and I dare not tell them, I was missing Storm. We stopped for food before heading home. I called Storm to see if he wanted anything to eat, but he said, "No," and I knew by that time he'd already eaten. I think the real reason I called was to try to get a feel for what kind of mood he was in.

About an hour passed before I was back at the house, and Storm was still wide awake watching television; but not much longer, the television was watching us as we just cuddled. We laughed and talked about my night. He saw Kimber's live video and he was glad I enjoyed myself. We talked into the early hours of the morning, just like old times. I was exactly where I wanted to be . . . in his arms. Sadly, the next few days those same strong, tattooed arms that held me, and those same hands that caressed me, would begin to push me away.

That Saturday was going to be a long day for Storm and I both. Keegan had a big game that required a road trip and Storm had to work at the store, he had band practice after that, and then plans with his family for his niece's birthday.

I was already tired from the late night, but I made my way to the kitchen to make breakfast for Storm and I before I headed to the game and him to work.

With my birthday and Thanksgiving being near, Teigan, Raigan and Klyde were already in town and they accompanied me to Keegan's game, just like old times. I was enjoying this time with them, especially since I didn't have to drive.

We really enjoyed the game and Keegan's team won. I was tired from all the yelling and coaching I did from the bleachers, not to mention, it was a particularly hot day for November. After the game, we were able to spend a little time with Keegan before he had to leave with his team, but he would be home in a few days.

Klyde drove us home from the game, and I loved the noise from the three of them making plans to go out later that night. I just thought to myself, *Oh, to be young again.* I was so exhausted from the past few days that sleep was falling down on me like rain. I just wanted a long, hot shower and a pillow! Once we were home, I got just what I wanted. After my shower, I laid on my couch and went right to sleep. I needed that.

Later that night when Storm called to tell me he was finally heading home, I could barely open my eyes, let alone move. Usually, I would've hopped up and went on over to Storm's place, but that night I decided to stay home. I could sense the hesitation in his voice as he said, "OK." As a matter of fact, I was still talking when I heard the dial tone. I thought, *Really? Did the call drop or did he hang up on me?* Honestly, at that point, I was too tired to even care, but I will say this, he didn't call back and neither did I.

Sunday was a typical day for me. I woke up early as usual, and by me being in my own home, I could move about without disturbing Storm. I read a little, I worked out, then washed clothes all before cooking breakfast for myself and the kids.

I let Storm sleep-in before calling him. He's not a morning person and I knew he also had a busy day ahead. I wanted him to get as much rest as possible. When we finally spoke, I could tell by his tone that he was feeling some type of way about the night before, but I didn't bite the bait. Yet he complained about every damn thing. I called him too early, he still needed to get his hair retwisted, he had band practice later, but one of the members wasn't going to be there, his grandson was having a birthday party and he still needed to get a gift; blah, blah, blah. At that point, I was fed up with the nagging. I wanted to yell, "Well, shut up and get moving!" Instead I sarcastically asked, "Is it your time of the month as well?" We both laughed. I only held back because I knew he had back-to-back shows on Monday and Tuesday nights. He needed my support, not my sass.

I went on about my day. The kids and I had dinner at my mom's. I was truly enjoying this time with them. I would still check in on Storm to make sure he didn't need anything. As the day was ending, I headed over to Storm's. He was so frustrated and stressed from his day that I only spent a few hours with him before heading home. When he got that way, he became very detached. I knew he would be restless, I knew everything I said, even in love, would come off as bothersome to him. I thought he needed to be alone; he needed some space. I wanted him to be in a better place mentally for his shows on Monday and Tuesday.

Early Monday morning Storm called and said he had a hard time sleeping without me being there. He even said he slept on my pillow so he could smell the coconut oil from my hair. I laughed, because I felt the same way, I missed sleeping next to him also. I was starting to feel like I couldn't live with him and I couldn't live without him. The relationship was starting to become a challenge, but I was down for the challenge. Storm would always say that most of his relationships didn't last long, and that at least we made it past three months. I would get offended when he said that, because I felt he was waiting for it to fail, or maybe he was waiting to use it as an excuse later down the road. He would also say that he was used to women leaving him when things got hectic. I wasn't that type of woman, and I definitely wasn't going to be her once he spoke that. I was determined to show him differently. I think that's where he hooked me and reeled me in. Thinking back, I should've asked him what his definition of "hectic" was.

The conversation became strange when Storm continued to say that he almost got up and drove past my house last night to make sure I was there. I was confused as hell, because the main reason I went home was because of his attitude. I didn't like the tone of the conversation, but I quickly told him the next time he feels that way, not to drive past but to come and knock. I had no secrets. I also told him he should have called me. We all have insecurities at times, and I didn't have any problems addressing his insecurities and moving forward, but he told me that it was an issue he needed to work out himself, and that it had nothing to do with me. I thought, *OK, fair enough.*

Later that evening after work, I got on the road and headed to Storm's show. Teigan, Raigan and Klyde rode with me, and Keegan met us there. They wanted to support Storm as well. I was thankful for them, because a lot of times I would be the only girlfriend at the shows. Sometimes Storm's mother, father, brother and one of his close friends would show up. The kids kept me company that night.

It was a really good show and we all enjoyed it. Storm dedicated the band's most requested song to me, "My Girl" by the Temptations. He even came off stage to dance with me a little during the band's rendition of Marvin Gaye's "Sexual Healing." Afterwards, we chatted with Storm and he introduced the kids to the band members. They all already knew me, but that night they weren't overly friendly towards me as they usually were.

I just remembered how good Storm smelled when he hugged me. As I placed a kiss on his neck, the kids yelled "Ewww!" We had a good laugh before departing our separate ways. I knew Storm would get in late after closing up after the performance. I wanted to enjoy my kids, so I decided I would just stay at home that night, but not before checking to see if Storm needed anything. He said he was good and that he didn't need anything. All of a sudden, I had a gut feeling that something wasn't right.

Tuesday morning started off as a usual day. I was up and out the door early for work. I sent Storm a quick text message to let him know I was thinking about him, even though I knew it would be a couple of hours before he would even wake up and see it.

Once he was up and going, I knew he would text back. This day, when he texted back, it was close to my break time, so I called him. He seemed distant and frustrated. I asked if he was ok? I then asked if we were ok? He said yes, and that he was just upset, because he felt he didn't have the community's support when it came to his business and to his shows. I was confused, because when he did get support, he would consider it "fake love." I also tried to get him some sponsors, but he never followed up. I was unsure of what he was trying to say, but I reminded him that he had the support of those who cared for him and loved him the most. His family supported him and his friends supported him. Hell, I bent over backwards to support him. Missing some shows or not buying something from the store everyday didn't mean that people didn't support him. Why was he seeking this outside validation from the community? He had somehow missed the big picture, and I felt he was being ungrateful. Even after that explanation from Storm about the frustration in his voice, I still felt something was off.

Instead of arguing with him, I just suggested that maybe he needed to take some time off from his band and the store just to clear his head. The headaches were increasing, the sinus issues wouldn't let up, his mood was unpredictable, and then he started complaining about a freaking toothache. He was taking pain pills for the headaches, pain pills for the toothache and almost every medicine possible for the sinus issues. The more I tried to convince him to see a doctor, the more he seemed to resent me. To me, he was spiraling down, and I began to worry about him, and so did one of his closest friends.

After hanging up from Storm, I confided in Katie about what was going on with him. I know she picks up on my demeanor and overhears my conversations, so she wasn't surprised at what I was telling her. She said she had been praying for me. I continued to tell her that I picked up on negative energy last night after the show. I wanted to make sure I wasn't just being sensitive or tripping because my cycle was on. She assured me that it wasn't that, and she said she could tell the honeymoon phase was over.

Yes, I admit, clouds were forming, but I didn't think it was anything Storm and I couldn't work through. Storm is a perfectionist and I knew he was under a lot of pressure. He was his own biggest critic, and for some reason he never felt he was good enough.

Katie agreed with my idea that maybe Storm needed a break. She also thought it would be a good idea if Storm and I took that break together. I agreed. I needed to unwind too.

I started brainstorming. I was trying to figure out something simple, but nice, to do. Then I remembered that Storm had mentioned more than once wanting to go to this jazz concert. It was local and was scheduled to take place a week before Christmas. That was perfect. I was thinking, *This would be so relaxing and would take his mind off of his chaotic life . . . even if only for a day.* I was going to make that day special. Besides, I felt we needed to reconnect. I needed some alone time with my man. Even though I saw him almost every day, I was missing him.

I was so excited as I logged onto the internet and started planning. First, I made dinner reservations at this romantic, upscale restaurant for after the jazz concert. I made sure they had duck and lamb on their menu, because I knew that's what he had been wanting for a while. Our taste in food was different, but I just made sure there was some type of chicken on the menu and I was good. The day was going to be all about Storm.

Next, I went on to purchase the concert tickets, and just like when Storm purchased tickets for us to go see the Jacksonville Jaguars, price wasn't an issue. I chose the best seats available. As soon as the transaction was complete, I received a text alert. I thought it was my E-tickets being sent, but it was a text message from Storm. I just smiled because I was just about to text him and surprise him with the information for our special day. I figured that would give him time to clear busy his schedule.

I was thinking how cute it was that we were thinking about each other at the same time. I was excited, I felt happy and felt like relief was on the way. That was until I actually opened the message. I reached up and grabbed my glasses, because clearly, I was not reading this correctly.

CHAPTER 3
BLINDSIDED

I gasped for air. It felt like I couldn't breathe. It felt like I had been sucker punched. Katie asked what was wrong. No words would form. For the first time in a long time, I was totally speechless, so I got up and handed her my phone. I became anxious as she read the text out loud. "I want to focus more on my music career. I can't balance a relationship, my store and the band right now. If I had to make a choice between my music career and you, I choose my music." *Huh? Choose? Who said he had to choose? Is this what he meant by music was his wife? Was he telling me then that me, nor our relationship, would ever be his main priority?*

I grabbed my phone from Katie and went outside to call Storm, because words were beginning to form, and I damn sure wasn't replying by text.

Storm answered the phone call as if he expected it, but had the nerve to say he was with a customer and couldn't talk. *Couldn't or wouldn't? I was done with being nice and understanding. Damn your customer. Stop hiding behind a text. What man sends his girlfriend a text like that while she's at work? Oh, hell no! He was not going to brush me off. This is some shit a coward does. I deserve an explanation and I want it now.* My mind was on overload and it wouldn't stop thinking just as my mouth wouldn't stop talking. *I'm tired of being the bigger person. I'm tired of biting my tongue. What about my feelings?*

I called Storm back and we talked until my mouth was dry, literally. Storm talked in circles about feeling inadequate as a man, said he felt he wasn't a good boyfriend and that he only knew how to be a husband. *A husband? Don't you have to be a boyfriend first? And haven't you had three tries at the husband thing?* What Storm was saying to me made no sense at all. All I heard was unweighted excuses of why he needed a break from us, from me.

I was so confused and emotional. My mind was all over the place. *A break?* He was the one who promised if we ever got mad at each other we would talk it out. We promised we'd never keep secrets from each other. I tried to be understanding, but by his nonchalant tone, he had that text planned out for a while now.

Keeping a rational perspective was hard, and I quickly became angry. I thought Storm was very inconsiderate. *What about my birthday plans? What about the Thanksgiving plans we had with his family? What about the concert tickets I had just purchased? What about the deposit he made on our summer vacation?* My thoughts wouldn't stop. I wanted to yell SHUT UP! I just needed to think clearly. Then, I started talking to myself.

Ok, relax Sydnee. Maybe Storm is just having a bad day. Maybe he's in a bad mood and just taking it out on you.

How did I miss the red flags? How in the hell did I not see this coming?

The pain, anger and confusion started flowing out through my eyes. Before I knew it, I was crying. I was so upset that I had to leave work.

I called Maya and told her everything. She was just as mad as I was. She said, "Syd, no the hell he didn't text you that shit!"

She continued, "Let's go to the store and whoop his ass!"

I tearfully laughed and said, "No, Maya," even though it sounded like a good idea.

Maya then said, "Let's at least go and flatten his tires!"

"No, Maya."

"Pour paint thinner on his car?!"

"MAYA, NO!!!"

She then told me she was leaving work also and for me to meet her for a drink. Lord knows I needed one.

On the way to meet Maya, I called Kimber and filled her in on the latest drama. She really didn't have much to say. My guess is she wasn't all that surprised, because I'm a hopeless romantic and she's a realist. Our expectations of men were different.

Stephanie's response was blunt, as expected. "That's just why I didn't want you getting back involved with his punk ass! He's a freaking joke!" Stephanie continued to say, "He better be glad I don't live there, because we'd go beat his ass." Stephanie even wanted his phone number; she said she had some things she wanted to say to him. I laughed. Of course I didn't give her his number; he wouldn't have been able to handle that mouth of hers.

When I talked to Frankie, she was so relaxed and very calm, but her response was the most powerful! "Syd, that's his loss. You are a queen with or without a king, so get yourself together. If he can just end it like that, he doesn't even deserve you anyways. You are too much of a woman to be half loved. You gave his ungrateful ass too much too soon and he couldn't handle that. You wear your heart on your sleeve and he took advantage of that, but he'll regret it." I was soaking up the encouraging words, and she continued to pour into me, "Your birthday dinner is coming up and we are going to enjoy ourselves like we normally do. You are better than this; you are stronger than this. You are going to be just fine. I love you, girl." At that point, I was crying like a baby.

Later that night, Storm and I talked before his show. He acted as if I had overreacted about his text. Well, that definitely proved my point about sending a text to begin with. He said he just needed time to think about things. I just couldn't figure out what things, and when I asked, he wouldn't communicate, not then, and just like he wouldn't in the past. He continued to say he didn't want to be accountable for my feelings. *What in the hell did that mean?* Whatever it meant, it was too damn late. My feelings were hurt and my heart was broken. I thought, *He needs to get him a mannequin, a blow-up doll, or a robot if he doesn't want to deal with feelings. What does he think happens in a relationship?*

Oh yea, I see what's happening. He wasn't ready for the new Sydnee. His ass is afraid of commitment. Did he not realize that pursuing a good woman will require him to be a good man? To be honest and consistent? Did he not realize in relationships you compromise and make sacrifices?

I thought I had pushed him away, but he was running from himself. There were parts of himself that he wasn't ready to expose. What I do know is the soul has no secrets that your behavior won't tell. It was all starting to come out, but for some strange reason, I was still willing to dumb myself down and was willing to compromise. I wanted to talk it out, to work it out. I wanted to figure it out. Maybe I just needed closure. Honestly, I didn't know what the hell I wanted, and that just left me more confused. I was lost. I was feeling unsure. I couldn't believe I loved him so much that even through my pain, I still tried to understand him. I was so damn determined to find an excuse for his behavior.

I remember my head hurting and my stomach cramping as I lay in bed and thought to myself, *How could Storm lay next to me almost every night for five months and think it's okay to walk away by a text? He said he loved me, said we were meant to be, begged me not to ever leave him. He said I was his lady and he wanted to marry me. I was building a bond with his son. Why didn't Storm just talk to me?*

Then, I began to question myself out loud. "*What did I miss? How could I lie next to someone almost every night for five months and not realize he had mentally detached from me and from the relationship? There was no way this just happened over night. When I asked him if anything was wrong between us, why didn't he speak up?*"

My mind starting racing again, and my thoughts became louder. *While I was looking for the best in him, he was looking for a way out.* As everything came flooding back to me, tears began to flow. I was mad, sad, bitter and confused. Then I turned that anger towards myself. *How could you be so stupid, Syd? Why did you even let him back in your life?* Everything was starting to come together. Everything was starting to make sense. Or was it? Or had his paranoia rubbed off on me? *Am I tripping? Nah Syd, you aren't tripping.*

The questions and thoughts in my head continued.

Did everyone but me know that something was wrong? Is that why the band members looked confused when I was at the show last night? Had he told them that he wanted to end things with me before he told me? Why didn't he communicate with me? Why didn't he talk to me about us? I even started to wonder if they encouraged him to leave me?

Then I thought back to a couple of nights after my vacation to Aruba, Storm's mother and I waited outside the venue after a show while the men packed up. When they finally came out, it was Storm, the band members, his brother and father. Storm hugged me then said, "I didn't know you were coming." I'm sure I looked shocked as hell, but I didn't respond. I don't know if it was because he was bold enough to lie to my face or what, but Storm and I talked while I was on the way to the show because he wanted to let me know he had already paid my cover charge. He knew damn well I was coming. Had he started lying on me and about me?

The questions in my head wouldn't stop.

Is that why his employee's girlfriend was posting subliminal messages on social media about dating and saying things like, "Know your place in a man's life?" Was that directed at me? Nah, it can't be. She's a woman and a Christian. She wouldn't intentionally bash or hurt another woman's feelings. Well, what about his cousin's wife who had posted, "If someone wants to walk away, let them"? Was that meant for me? Did he tell them he wanted to walk away? Nah, as a woman she knows what heartbreak feels like. She wouldn't have been that insensitive.

At that point, I was being so sensitive to every post and comment on social media. I was reading deep into everything. I was reading between the lines, finding things that probably weren't even there. That did teach me to be careful what I post, because we don't know what people are really going through behind closed doors. From that day on, I learned to keep my social media posts positive or funny.

Yes, it's social media and we can post what we want to, but I decided to try and stay away from anything that would inadvertently hurt or shame someone. I think we fail to realize that most of the time, it's not what we say, but it's how we say it, or when we say it, that matters the most.

I also vowed to practice what I post and use my page to inspire other women, not belittle them, not throw shade at them when I know they are going through something. I also realized we need to be more supportive, kind and loving women. To be the ones who aren't afraid to be transparent about life. The ones who will guide you when you're travelling down a road they've already travelled. Be the ones that uplift, empower and encourage. To be the queens who will straighten your crown when your head is down. And I was starting with myself. I vowed to be the change I wanted to see.

Even if we don't agree, we just have to learn to be empathetic to other women and stop competing, stop gossiping and start praying. We need to stop being catty. Stop assuming, stop judging her based on the opinions of others and get to know her for yourself. That attitude she had when you ran into her at work, in the store, or in the hair salon, had nothing to do with you, but everything to do with her. Maybe it was her relationship failing or her kids running wild. Maybe she could be grieving or she's having financial problems or she's exhausted from taking care of a sick parent, child or spouse. Invite her out to lunch; better yet, invite her on your next girls' trip. Suggest an encouraging book for her to read. Send her a positive text message. Show her you care.

I also learned that everyone is different and we handle issues differently. I won't ever tell someone how or when to get over something I've never personally been through. I dare not judge a person, nor will I laugh for the way they handle their pain, their stress or their hurt and heartbreak. No matter what your current status is, whether you're married, widowed, divorced, single, or dating, *every* woman has possibly been used, broken, lied to, misled, confused, rejected, abandoned, mistreated, embarrassed or played by someone they loved, cared for or trusted. Some may have even forgiven that person and are currently in a relationship with them.

I gave my heart to Storm, and when I did, I no longer guarded it. I trusted him with it and it was his to protect, but he didn't. I don't regret loving him the way I did. I don't regret loving hard. His actions define him.

They don't define me. I sure wish I had known all this back then, because I felt small, I felt dumb and I felt stupid. According to society, I should have known better. And when you're hurting, that's the last thing you want to hear, along with, "I told you so."

I read something recently on a sponsored page on social media. It was entitled, "Never Diminish Your Relationship Failures," and I wish I had seen it sooner, because it really put a lot of things into perspective.

Nonetheless, at the time, I felt betrayed. I felt let down. Why wasn't Storm just straight up with me about what was really going on? I had this gut feeling it was a lot more than about his music career.

Confident as I was, there I was feeling unloved, unwanted. I felt insecure and like I had been taken advantage of. I started to let petty people and things get to me.

I continued to ponder and to beat myself down and the questions continued. *Why didn't I question him when things didn't sit right with me? Why didn't I question him the way he questioned me? Why didn't I speak up for myself when he said or did things I didn't like? Why didn't I leave when I started to feel uncomfortable in his home after him telling me, "People like you who wake up early and happy make me sick"?* Instead, I chose him over my morning prayer and daily devotional reading time. I stopped doing my morning routine in order to keep from making any noise. Instead, I would have everything ready for the next day the night before. In the morning once I woke up, I would quietly get out the bed, go straight to the bathroom, shower, get completely dressed, do my hair and when I emerged from the bathroom, all I had to do was kiss him goodbye, grab my purse and leave. How did I not see this? I guess it's true when they say, "When God doesn't have your attention, he'll disturb what does."

The thoughts and questions continued in my head.

THROUGH THE STORM

Was Storm trying to make me jealous or feel insecure when he said that a lot of women were throwing themselves at him and making sexual advances toward him once they knew he was in a relationship? It was hard to decipher between a lie and the truth, because it was hard to believe that grown ass women would really act like that. I see it like this: a woman that'll cheat with you will also cheat on you. Is that the type of woman he wanted? The crazy part is that I think he enjoyed the attention. All that had done was fuel his ego while destroying mine.

Was it true when Storm said that one young lady I knew started bringing him lunch to the store? But, wait . . . did he accept the lunch? Did he not tell her that I prep his lunch on Sundays for the week?

Was he trying to make me mad when he said a few of his exes started reaching out to him? The conversation that stood out the most was when Storm told me that one of his exes had started coming into the store a lot lately shopping for her young grandson. I quickly replied, "I wish I would catch her desperate ass in there." He laughed at first, until I continued, "As much as you're in that store working, stocking and cleaning, how in the hell did you forget there's no children's section?!"

I remember him smirking one night as he told me that one of his ex-wives had called and asked if he needed help working in the store, even though she knew he was in a relationship with me and that I helped in the store already. I asked him why they still communicated, especially since they had no kids together. He just laughed and claimed she was trying to butter him up, because she wanted him to help get her daughter into a private school where one of his friends worked in admissions.

He even told me that one of his good friends had come into the store and asked him what I had that she didn't. He just laughed it off and said, "Syd, she's like the sister I never had and I've never seen her in any other way." None of that bothered me when he was telling me then, but as I replayed it, I was fuming. I was hot and heated and not in a good way. If they were such good friends, she would have respected his relationship. Hell, if he were a good man, he would have respected our relationship.

Who would purposely flirt with, or try to seduce a man knowing he's in a relationship? I've seen the women who are bold enough to wink their eyes or lick their lips at a man while he's with his woman. At first, I would think that was confidence, but when it happens to you, you look at the situation through a different lens. But now, through my own healing, I realized it's not confidence. It's weakness, low self-esteem, insecurities and hurt pouring out in the form of promiscuity.

All the pillow talk we shared, and all the innocent conversations we had were beginning to look like Storm was intentionally trying to make me self-conscious about myself and our relationship.

That hurt bad. I felt wounded. The things he said about the other women started to stick to me like glue and I started thinking, *I will never, ever entertain a man that has a wife or girlfriend. I would never interfere with anyone's relationship. I never want to be the reason another woman feels the way I'm feeling now. I never want to be the reason a woman lays alone at night crying about her man. I don't want anyone hurting like this because of me. Wait . . . is this my karma? Is this payback from my past? Lord, I apologize to any woman I've ever hurt. I apologize to anyone I've ever been toxic toward. I know in my younger days, I was the cause of a few broken hearts. Lord, please forgive me.*

I remember him laughing while showing me his phone one day, because one of his ex-mothers-in-law sent him a friend request on social media. This was the same lady who had shown up as a suggested friend on my page as well. What was so interesting about our social media pages?

Things started making sense. I was starting to figure out what was going on. I mean, I think I was. I started to question his motives. *While Storm was the one who suggested we post on social media, why was that now his biggest complaint?*

Was he lying when he said one of his ex-girlfriends was so upset about our posts that she threatened suicide? I remember my high school boyfriend telling me that same pathetic lie so I wouldn't tell anyone about us. Even though I thought Storm was possibly lying, I asked him why would he even allow someone that unstable access to his social media page and why in the hell were they even still talking? But, I got a blank stare. Storm seemed to be able to communicate with everyone else just fine, but when it came to me, you could hear crickets.

Was he not man enough to say, "Yes, I have a girlfriend, and yes, she'll mind if we exchange numbers" or "yes, she'd mind if we are still communicating" or "no, thanks, Sydnee packs my lunch" or "no, thank you, Sydnee helps me in the store."

I couldn't let this go. I continued to try to figure that social media shit out. *What was it? Did Storm finally get the attention he wanted, but couldn't handle it? Did he finally catch 'her' eye and wanted to spare 'her' feelings at the cost of mine? How could I build with him if he still craved attention from other women?* I spoke life into him every chance I got, and I catered to his needs, but he still was seeking outside validation.

Wait a minute! This is starting to come together! My mind went back to mid-September. Storm's family had big plans for his father's retirement party. I was unable to attend due to Keegan having an out-of-state game in which my flight and hotel were already booked and paid for. Storm tried to convince me not to go to Keegan's game, but instead to accompany him, but I didn't. I wouldn't dare. I would have lost more than my money for the flight and hotel. I would have lost Keegan's respect.

Nonetheless, I helped Storm prepare for his father's big weekend by picking up his tuxedo from the cleaners. I also picked up his watch that needed repairing from the jeweler. Once home that evening, as Storm and I went through his closet to determine the shoes he should wear to his father's retirement celebration, he turned to me and said, "I really wish you were going with me, Syd." I hugged him and said, "I know, me too. I was really looking forward to meeting the rest of your family, especially your other two sons." Storm continued to say, "You just don't know how many people I planned on making mad this weekend after I posted our pictures!" I can't believe how I let comments like that go over my head.

Then more questions arose, questions I should have been asking Storm and myself. How many recent exes does he have? I mean, other than the three ex-wives that I know about. How many baby mommas does he really have? How many friends with benefits has he had lately? How many sexual partners has he had? Why can't he keep a serious relationship? How many lives has he ruined and how many hearts has he broken?

The day Storm and I made the verbal commitment to each other by vowing to be faithful and to be truthful, open and honest, he jokingly said he'd give me time to "clean house," referring to any exes I needed to "get rid of." Apparently, the joke was on him. Storm was the one who seemed to have unfinished business and a lot of it.

Were people really talking to him about my social media or were the "he," "she" and "they" really him and his guilt and insecurities or was he just playing mind games with me? Did Storm really just want to taunt me?

Over the next few days, it was a whirlwind of emotions. There were a lot of tearful, explosive phone calls, texts and emails exchanged between Storm and me. I was losing control. I felt defeated as I tried to reason with him, as I tried to get an explanation from him. I wanted my irrational thoughts to be silenced, so I wanted the truth from him. I wanted the truth and a damn apology. I deserved it, but Storm was not sorry, nor compassionate. It was like I didn't know him anymore.

Just like my retirement plan at work, I was vested in this relationship and was not letting it go without a fight! I really wanted to know what was going on with Storm. So, I tried to guilt him, seduce him, shame him; I tried to be nice, act weak and submissive, then I cursed him out. But Storm wasn't giving up any real information. Just more lies and excuses. I was so mad at Storm. I loved him, wanted to slap him, needed a hug from him, was disappointed in him and wanted to be lying next to him all at the same damn moment. Yet, he was so cold and heartless. He showed no emotion and he just couldn't seem to understand mine. Hell, I couldn't understand my emotions and no one who's never walked in my shoes will ever understand my emotions. Storm was the cause of all this pain and he had the audacity to brush me off then judge me at my lowest. I was now thinking like Maya. *Maybe I should go over there and beat his ass.* At this point, my boys wanted to also.

The questions and thoughts continued.

We made a commitment to each other. How dare he just walk away after all I sacrificed, after all I did to make this work. I put so much time and effort into this. Lord, is that why I'm fighting so hard to fix this? Can it even be fixed? Is it worth being fixed? If I win this fight, is it really a win? What am I fighting for anyway? To be half loved? To be ignored? I lowered my standards for him. I then realized that you will never be able to please an ungrateful person.

What in the hell is going on? What's wrong with you, Syd? My mind wouldn't let me sleep. Nothing seemed to help. I even got up and made myself a hot cup of chamomile tea to calm my nerves, as I so often did for Storm when he was restless, but there was no one there to rub my back and tell me everything would be okay.

The thoughts in my head bounced around like kids on a trampoline.

Perhaps Storm realized he wasn't ready for a relationship. Maybe he realized he's not worthy or deserving of my love. Did he not heal from his last divorce? Then the thought crossed my mind that maybe he hadn't healed from his first divorce, causing the other two marriages to fail, as well as causing his other relationships to fail, causing him to feel inadequate as a man.

I should've known it was too good to be true. But God, I prayed for this. I prayed for Storm, I prayed for us. Storm said he prayed for this, for me, for us.

Then I asked myself out loud, *"Did you really fall for this shit, again?"* Lord, I'm so confused right now. I don't know what to do.

> "Alone in a room
> It's just me and you
> I feel so lost
> 'Cause I don't know what to do
> Now what if I choose the wrong thing to do
> I'm so afraid, afraid of disappointing you.
> So I need to talk to you
> And ask you for your guidance
> Especially today
> When my mind is so cloudy
> Guide me until I'm sure
> I open up my heart.

"OPEN MY HEART" BY YOLANDA ADAMS

Over the next week or so, the girls tried to comfort me and make sense of it all too. They were just as confused as I was with all of this. With Maya being a social worker and Stephanie a nurse, they asked me if I thought Storm was maybe bipolar, depressed or suffered from anxiety. At this point, anything seemed likely to me, but through my pain, I replied back maybe he's just unhappy with himself and that's why he's so unsettled, disconnected and always frustrated. Seriously though, if what the girls suggested were true, that surely wouldn't have made any difference to me in my relationship with Storm. I truly loved Storm and already knew a little about his past and that didn't change my feelings towards him, even though I was starting to believe he had kept things from me.

What bothers me is the fact that people aren't honest about the demons they are currently fighting. If you're embarrassed to be upfront about your mental health, then you are around the wrong people or maybe you haven't completely embraced and accepted yourself yet. We all have baggage, but we must be willing to communicate that. We have to be adult enough to unpack that shit right in front of each other, discuss it, talk about it, figure it out and build each other up.

We need to be real and be honest, and let people know what it is or what it isn't. Give them a fair chance in the fight.

I'll even accept the insecurities, but I need your trust. Let me know what I'm working with so we can work on it together to make each other better. Until we're honest about our issues, we can't heal and move forward. We have to be willing to outgrow our pain, not use it as an excuse.

We also need to end the stigma about mental health. As a matter of fact, going to a therapist when you're feeling low or overwhelmed, anxious, stressed or depressed is just as important as going to your primary care doctor when you're sick. People will work so hard to hide the truth about themselves from others, but won't work hard to get themselves help in order to get better.

I don't know exactly what it was with Storm, but trying to figure it all out had me looking unstable. Yet, I think that's what he wanted. Now that I'm on the outside looking in, it feels like gaslighting. He had manipulated me so much and I was so in love that I hadn't even noticed.

A few days later, Stephanie emailed me the signs of depression:

Sadness * tiredness * trouble focusing or concentrating * unhappiness * anger * irritability * frustration * loss of interest in pleasurable or fun activities * sleep issues (little or too much) * no energy * craving unhealthy food * anxiety * isolation

With me still being mad and hurt and knowing what I dealt with behind closed doors, as well as being tired of people giving Storm an excuse for his behavior, in return, I emailed her the signs of a narcissist:

Nothing is their fault * their way or the highway * you work overtime on the relationship, while they don't work on it at all * they are never there for you emotionally * they are blind to your emotions, love, accomplishments, needs and pain * loses interest as the expectation of intimacy increases or when they've won at their game * many have trouble sustaining a relationship for more than six months

Frankie suggested that maybe Storm was intimidated by me. Even though I thought she was partially right, I thought, *But, how? Why?* He's the one who came knocking down my door. He said my strong personality is what attracted him to me. He said he liked my sense of style and the way I took care of and supported my children. He loved the way I was family-oriented and the way I worked hard. He said he loved the fact that I was travelling and enjoying life and that he couldn't wait until we were able to travel together. He said he liked the way I made plans and was so attentive to detail. According to him, I was his dream girl. So, how could the same thing that caught his eye not keep his heart? I guess the same way having a good heart can be a blessing and a curse.

Was he looking for love, but just not ready for love?

Thanksgiving came and it was awkward. No one verbally asked, but facial expressions and whispers yelled, "Where is Storm?" or "I thought she was spending Thanksgiving with Storm and his family?"

My birthday came and I truly enjoyed myself. My family and friends wouldn't have it any other way. They weren't going to settle for anything less and we definitely weren't going to let one monkey stop the show. Stephanie even flew into town and surprised me. On the way home from my dinner, she plugged up her phone and went down her play list and said, "This song is dedicated to Storm's punk ass." It was one of Ella Mai's songs and it damn sure wasn't "Boo'd up," instead it was "Don't want you." Frankie said, "Yasssssss!" Maya said, "Since we're all together, this will be a good time to pull up on Storm and beat his ass!" Kimber and I laughed uncontrollably! That was the hardest I laughed in a long time!

> "What you talkin' 'bout you changed your mind? Didn't I
>   treat you right?
> Find your way to my heart now you putting on like you
>   don't
> Want to be around, can't spend much time
> Boy you better recognize
> Little money in your pocket, now you're tricking

Talking to me like you're winning

I was there when you needed me the most so I'm in my
feelings, I'm ashamed of the way I felt and you know it's
killing my pride.

Wasting my time, ain't no surprise.

You're the last one that's for real. I guess you learn and you
live.

It was now mid-December and the date of the jazz concert came so quickly. Even though I sold the tickets at full price a few weeks earlier, I cried and cried the whole day. I just knew that would be the day we reconnected. Why didn't he hold on? Why didn't he fight for me? For us? Instead of trying to work on our issues together, why did he become so damn defensive?

At work, our year-end staff meeting was incorporated with our Christmas party and guess who's note was the first pulled from the happy jar? Yes, mine. Thank God I never put my name on it, but I still felt embarrassed. I kept quiet. People were looking around and saying, "Aww, I hope they are still together." Little did they know, just as sure as the year was ending, so had my relationship with Storm.

Valentine's Day came and went and I received a box of chocolates from a male coworker who was always very nice to me. I received an edible arrangement from a close friend whom I had distanced myself from at the request of Storm. My kids even treated me like royalty. They had roses, balloons and chocolate covered strawberries delivered to my job and they all surprised me and came to town just to take me to dinner, but I still cried and cried and cried.

A heartbreak doesn't care about your age, your race, or how educated you are. It doesn't care how rich you are, how good of a person you are. The shit is painful, and I was going through something I had never been through before. I had been in other relationships before, but this was the first one I truly gave my all to. That's why I couldn't understand why it failed and that's why it was so hard to walk away. I opened up to Storm completely and trusted him with my deepest secrets. I trusted him with my heart, mind, body and soul, and that's probably why it hurt so bad.

I remember reaching out to a few older women. Women that were more seasoned, had more experience and wisdom than me. I wanted their opinion and input. I wanted to make sense of this, but nothing seemed to help.

I even reached out to a friend of Storm's who I happened to know personally. That conversation left me more hurt and confused, because I could tell by his tone that Storm had told him way more than he had told me. What was Storm hiding? Why didn't he come to me about our problems?

The days were passing slowly. My mind would drift back and forth. I tried to forget about Storm, but I was missing him. Simple things, like a romantic movie on Lifetime or a certain song on the radio, would cause me to cry. Although the questions in my head slowed up, they were still there. I was being so hard on myself. I was blaming myself. *Could I have done more? What did I do wrong? What could I have done differently? Should I keep trying? Why did he do me like that?*

Then finally it happened. I asked myself the most important question of all. *Why did you allow him to do you like that?*

I thought back to a day when I was listening to the radio at work and the topic was based on a recent study that said something about "the person who loves the least in a relationship controls the relationship." I remember spinning around and asking Katie what she thought about it and she disagreed with it. I disagreed with it at first, but as I listened more, I began to see where the speaker was coming from. That night, as I replayed it in my head, I realized that lately there had been a lot of unmatched efforts going on between us. I couldn't figure out when I lost him. I couldn't figure out where my trying to make it work, or me trying to help him, turned into me chasing him. One thing I do know is if the study was right, at that point, I loved Storm a lot more than he loved me.

I then realized that I was caught up in my feelings. I let my emotions cloud my judgment. I clearly wasn't myself. I was starting to relate to and understand Lynn Whitfield's character in "Thin Line Between Love and Hate." The movie is about an observable, fast-talking party man and player, Darnell Wright, who finally gets his punishment when one of his conquests takes his actions personally, and comes back for revenge.

My thoughts weren't my thoughts. In that moment, I admit I had temporarily lost my way. I knew my worth, so why was I trying to make Storm love me? Why did I feel the need to be accepted by him? I surely learned the hard way that you have to train your mind to be stronger than your emotions or you'll lose yourself each time. And, I was losing big time. I was emotionally, physically and mentally tired. I couldn't figure out what caused the temporary melt down. My loyalty to Storm and my common sense definitely weren't agreeing.

I began to feel so bad as a mother also, because Raigan started having marital problems and I had no energy to comfort her. I definitely had no positive advice to give her either.

I then thought back to Frankie, and I said to myself, "Syd, you are a queen, now get yourself together." *How could I forget that I'm a queen? If Storm were meant for me, I wouldn't have to chase him or compete for him. Just because Storm didn't see my worth didn't mean I was worthless. Storm thinks he played me, but he played himself right out of a good woman.*

I then picked up my crown and decided I would move forward and work on myself and get my life together, instead of trying to work on and fix a grown ass man.

CHAPTER 4
SOUL SEARCHING

It's hard to let go, whether it's grief, guilt or shame, anger, bitterness or betrayal, loss, regret or love. Change is difficult, but so is remaining in the same unchanging place. Do you hold on or do you let go?

"Years of low self-esteem and insecurities
Church taught me how to shout and how to speak in tongues,
But preacher teach me how to live now when the tongue is done,
 help me
Shout, shout. Let it all out.
These are the things I can do without, so come on.
I'm talking to you, so come on.
See I, See I, I just wanna let it go, just wanna let it go, just let it go.
Jesus, please on my knees can't You hear me crying.
You said to put it in Your hands, and Lord, I'm really trying."

"LET IT GO" BY KIRK FRANKLIN

I needed to do a self-evaluation. I needed to do a mirror check. I started asking myself several questions.

Did I need to stop by the Potter's House? Did I need to be fixed? In order to fix something, it would first have to be broken. Was I broken? Is this why I seem to attract broken men or is it my aura of healing that attracts them? Is it the way I love hard and nurture? Is it my kind, giving heart?

Was I projecting? Was Storm projecting? Were we blaming each other for our past hurt and old heartbreaks? Did the conflict with Storm trigger unresolved issues from my past?

Did Storm really break me or did he just expose what I had covered up? I spent two years alone, focused on myself, but did I really heal?

"Healing begins where the wound was made."

ALICE WALKER

I needed to understand the true source of my pain. What was causing me to have this unhealthy attachment to someone who I know is toxic to me? What deep hurt was I harboring that allowed me to put up with Storm's treatment or the treatment of any other man that had been in and out of my life? Why did I feel that I somehow deserved this pain?

One night as I was drinking a glass of wine and watching a movie about a faithful wife who became enraged once she found out she had been betrayed by her devious husband, I began to cry. The movie was "Acrimony." That was my second time watching it, but this time I cried because I could see myself becoming like Taraji P. Henson's character, and Lord knows, I didn't want that. The love I had for Storm was turning into ill feelings, hostility and animosity. I couldn't believe I let Storm take me there! Even though I thought the wife's actions were wrong in the movie, I was one teardrop away from showing up at Storm's place and causing a scene. I wanted to inflict pain on him. I wanted him to feel the same hurt he had caused me. I wanted him to suffer mentally and physically. At that point, I knew I needed to bounce back, because I wouldn't look good in an orange jumpsuit, and although I own a pair of purple furry handcuffs, I'd never been to jail.

At that point, I started to replay every traumatic experience I've had. The experiences that happened to me and around me. The experiences that took a little piece of me when they happened.

True healing can get very ugly. It requires complete honesty with yourself. It was time for me to look deeper than the surface. I owed it to myself.

The first person I thought about was my best friend of over 20 years. She was the one who knew everything about me and still loved and accepted me. She was the one I had confided in since our elementary days at Pineda School. She was the one who I could no longer turn to or confide in anymore. All I could think about was how I watched her suffer for weeks and then slowly die without being able to do anything about it. She was so beautiful inside and out. She had been so full of life. To then see her lifeless was just heartbreaking. Jesus.

The last good memory I have to hang onto took place a week before she went into the hospital. We went out to celebrate my birthday. This is another reason why my birthday is special to me and why I celebrate hard. We had a great time that night; it was almost like she knew it would be our last fun night together. We danced, we sang. On the way home, we sang loud in the car, being each other's back up, being a duo. It was funny. We talked about everything and everybody. We had an amazing time. It would be that same night that she took sick and never recovered.

God, I miss her. It's been nine years. Why does it feel like yesterday? Is it that I regret never telling her goodbye? I sat with her all day, knowing it may be her last day, and I said nothing. I was too stubborn to let her go, but she left anyway. Did she know that I loved her? How dare she leave me? She was like my soulmate, and closer to me than a sister; she was my girl. I wasn't ready for her to go.

I remember speaking at her funeral and saying that you have to truly get to know someone before you can love or hate them, and I'm so glad I gave her a fair chance, because we became inseparable.

At least she left behind one child. My godson. He was my lifeline to her. He reminded me so much of her. But, seven years after she died, he died in a tragic accident. My God, at the age of 17 his life was snatched away from him. He was snatched away from me and my kids. It was hard holding myself together, but I knew I had to hold my kids up. This shook up my entire household and none of us would ever be the same. Man, he was so smart and vibrant, just like his mom. I wish I could've saved him. Why do I feel so guilty?

Am I feeling guilty for not completely forgiving my dad before he died a few years ago? I mean, he felt the need to apologize for not being a good father to me when I was a child, but I questioned why he waited to do it until he was on his deathbed. I felt as if he was trying to make me forgive him. He had plenty of times to tell me prior to that. Like during the last three years of his life while I was taking care of him. Yes I know, he was young when I was born, but so was my mother and she stepped up to the plate. I know he still had some maturing to do, but that didn't lessen the hurt. How could a man be OK with taking care of only some of his kids? How could a man only go and visit some of his kids and act like the others don't exist?

I remember several years back, I had been content with the fact that I had a boyfriend I called big daddy, and I had a sugar daddy, both while still dealing with my baby daddy. I had three men who still didn't equal a whole man to me. Was that because I wasn't whole or complete as a person yet? Was it because of the love and attention I never received from my real dad?

Yes, dad was torn between us kids and our mothers. There were seven of us and none of us had the same mother. I was the oldest and only girl. Maybe that's why he depended on me so much to handle his medical care. I understand now why he couldn't be there for me as much as I wanted him to be, but I was stubborn just like him. I held back. I tried to show no emotion even as he took his last breath. Deep inside I was hurting because I wanted to forgive him. I think I did, but I was determined to tell him on my own time, but he died before I told him. It almost reminded me of the situation with my best friend. Maybe I was hoping he wouldn't die; but he left me, too.

Once he died, I went into business mode. I was planning and preparing his final arrangements. I couldn't grieve. I wouldn't grieve. I dare not grieve. I was too stressed and overwhelmed to even feel anything other than sympathy for myself and anger. I was feeling unappreciated. I started to pull back from my paternal side of the family. I just wanted it all to be over and then I'd be done with them as well.

I was numb. I started being resentful and bitter. I started treating my brothers badly and they had nothing to do with what our father had done or not done. Lord, I was so selfish and such a hypocrite. I wanted forgiveness from the Lord for my sins, but I wouldn't forgive my own sick father.

What broke my heart even more was one day I was telling my mother how I felt about this whole situation and she revealed to me that my father had called her before he died. He apologized to her for not being in my life when I was a child. He also thanked her for raising me in the manner that she did. He told her if it hadn't been for my upbringing, I would not have been there for him, even though he wasn't there for me. I started to cry. She continued to say that before they ended the call, he told her he was proud of me and proud of the woman I had become. My God. That destroyed me. I just want to hug him and tell him I loved him and that I accepted his apology, but I couldn't now.

Why am I always trying to hold onto people?

Am I still hurting because I never grieved the baby I miscarried at the age of 14? I felt like I shouldn't cry. I was too young to understand why. Maybe I thought that if I cried, people would think that I wanted the baby. So, I hid my feelings. Although the pregnancy was unplanned, she was still my baby; and yes, I already loved her. Up to this day, I wonder what she would have been like. Back then people were taught to survive, not to heal. So, no one mentioned the baby ever again and I just tucked away her sweet little memory in my heart. I think that's why I'm so attached to Teigan, Raigan, Keegan and Klyde.

After coming to grips with the miscarriage, I decided to tell the twins about it. Raigan smiled and said, "We're rainbow babies," but Teigan quickly corrected her and said, "No, I'm the oldest, so I'm the rainbow baby." I just laughed. In my eyes, they are both my rainbow babies. It's true that God will bless you with more than you lost. The twins came at the right time. They changed my life. Because of them, I gained enough strength and courage to leave their abusive father. I wasn't about to let him harm them.

I know I healed from the physical bruises, but did I ever completely heal from the emotional abuse I secretly accepted from him? Why didn't I seek counseling or confide in someone? Why didn't I seek treatment for the post-partum depression I suffered after having the twins? I was so young, and all I remember is being embarrassed and feeling helpless.

THROUGH THE STORM

Why do I always feel embarrassed about what someone else did to me? For the pain, trauma, heartache and grief they caused me?

Did I ever forgive the guy that molested me when I was only 13? But how could I forgive him when all I wanted to do was just bury what happened? I never told a soul. If I would have, maybe I wouldn't have had to watch my back, thinking he would molest me again. Maybe if I would have, he would have went to jail. Instead, he went on to get married and raise a family. Has he molested another little girl?

All of this was becoming so intense, but I knew I needed to reach deep down and pull out everything that was hurting me, hindering me and haunting me. All those suppressed memories were very uncomfortable to relive, but it was what I needed. The Lord knows I wanted to know what was keeping me from a complete healing. I was determined to change. I wanted to do better, to be better and maybe then I'd attract better. I needed to break the curse.

> "The enemy is trying to make me believe
> That my past is who I am.
> That the mistakes I made from yesterday
> Is all that I would ever be.
> They told me I would be nothing.
> Nobody in my family ever was.
> They said you're just like your momma,
> Just like your daddy.
> Never amounted to anything.
> But that's not me, that's not who I am.
> God gave me a promise, on that I stand.
> The curse is broken

My past can't hold me

I'm more than a conqueror

That's what he told me

The curse is broken

My body's healed

The devil's a liar

It's in His will.

The mistake, is not who I am

The lies they told, is not who I am

My past, is not who I am

The curse is broken in my life.

The abortion, is not who I am

The misfortune, is not who I am.

The disease, is not who I am

The curse is broken in my life."

"THE CURSE IS BROKEN"

BY JAMES FORTUNE & FIYA

Through all of this, I kept remembering something my mom had said to me. "Syd, it's OK to want to be better and do better, but don't change who you are. Keep being the good person you are and the right one will love you just as you are." Katie, who went through everything with me because we shared a small office space, kept saying, "There's nothing wrong with you Syd, it's him." Yes, at first I was trying to change so Storm would love and accept me. But at this point, no one understood that it was deeper than that. The tears I shed weren't because of Storm. This wasn't about Storm anymore. It wasn't about someone else loving me. I wanted to make sure I loved myself. This journey was personal. It was about Sydnee McCullen.

Through the Storm

It was time to get to work. I was going to get to the root of my problems. No matter how painful it was, and no matter who caused the hurt and pain, it was up to me to heal and I was all in. I will tell you this, I was my toughest critic, but it was time to let go of my past, my hurt, my anger, my regrets, resentment and bitterness. It was time to be genuinely happy.

> "I couldn't seem to fall asleep
> There was so much on my mind
> Searching for that peace
> But peace I could not find
> So then I knelt down to pray
> Praying help me please
> Then He said you don't have to cry
> 'Cause I'll supply all your needs
> As soon as I stopped worrying
> Worrying how the story ends
> I let go and I let God
> Let God have his way"
>
> **"Let Go" by Dewayne Woods**

I limited my time on social media, and I cut back on watching television. I started listening again to strictly gospel music daily, not just on church days. I started following Sarah Jakes Roberts and Pastor TD Jakes on social media. I also followed Pastor Michael Todd and Steve Furtick. I started reading my daily devotional books again. I actually took on reading as my new pastime. The kids noticed that and purchased *Becoming* by Michelle Obama for me. That was the first book I enjoyed reading cover to cover.

I was just trying to soak up anything positive, inspirational and encouraging. That also led me to order *Healing the Soul of a Woman* by Joyce Meyer. It was so helpful to me, that I shared it with Maya once I was finished with it. I also ordered the study guide for myself, and I referred it to Frankie as well. It was like I had homework every night, but anything that kept me occupied and on the right path was worth it.

In Chapter 5, the Study Guide suggested taking a personality test to get to know yourself better. I did it and when I glanced at the results, I didn't really think it revealed anything new to me. I got the letters "ENFJ," which stood for extraverted, intuitive, feeling, judging. I already knew I was ambitious, but my ambition isn't self-serving. Yes, I'm charming and a strong humanitarian. Yep, that's me. Always trying to help some damn body. I didn't care to read any further.

Chapter 7 was "Hurting People Hurt People." In this chapter, I began to piece together some things. I began to understand people and their "whys." Some things were starting to make sense to me. Instead of being angry at Storm, I started to feel sorry for him. The fact that I was still trying to make excuses for him began to really weigh in on me too. It led me to more questions. *Is he afraid to let me in? Is that why every time we would get close and things were going good, he'd push me away? Is it hard for him to completely love me because he hasn't completely unloved everyone from his past? Has he let go of all unhealthy attachments to people, places, things and habits? Why didn't he trust me?* Wow, I wondered who had hurt him so badly that he's willing to sabotage anything good that was happening in his life. You definitely can't give a person a blessing they aren't ready to receive, even if you feel like you are the blessing.

After reading that chapter and doing the study guide, it made me want to reach out to Storm, so I did. I was already looking for a reason to call him and this was it. I apologized to him for my actions and my words during the ending of our relationship. I told him I forgave him as well, even though he never apologized. I even expressed to him the things from my past in hopes he'd open up as well, but his voice was dry. It seemed like what I entrusted him with went in one ear and out the other. The little bit he did hear, he in return used it against me. At that point, it dawned on me that you really don't know how damaged a person is until you try to love them, so I stopped taking the things he said and did so personal and kept moving forward. But talking to him and hearing his voice did open me up again and left me wondering if we'd reconcile our differences.

Also, I remembered something my cousin, Nan, said one night as we were driving home from Teigan and Raigan's birthday dinner. She said, "If you love him, stop talking about him or the situation, stop posting about it and just pray for him. Give him to God, Syd." That night, I did just that. That night I prayed and cried out for Storm.

The chapter also led me to apologize to a friend, who was also my travel partner, whom I had unintentionally hurt. I had been really upset at Storm, but I took it out on her. I let my sharp tongue take over that day and I still can't believe how I acted.

I also reached out to my cousin, Nicole. We were once so close, but I cut her off after my dad's funeral. I let my emotions take over and she probably didn't even know why I stopped talking to her. Nicole and I met and talked at our grandmother's house, who I hadn't seen in a while either, because I didn't want to run into Nicole over there. We cleared up a lot of things and then we planned to meet for dinner and drinks a few weeks later. During that time, we caught up and talked like old times. I filled her in on the situation between Storm and I. She offered advice and referred a self-love book that she was reading. I couldn't wait to get to the store and buy it, because I welcomed anything that would help me make sense of what and how I was feeling.

From that night on, we moved forward and left the past in the past. She's been such a positive force in my life since then. Her compassionate ear was something much needed at that exact point in my life. We were encouraging and lifting each other up. Supporting each other in our endeavors. We were pushing each other to do and be better. We were two women evolving. Which became the perfect name for her nonprofit organization.

I was telling a coworker about Nicole's nonprofit organization and that she was interested in speaking at the next event, a women's empowerment brunch titled "Behind the Lipstick, What's Your Shade?" That led us to talking about the issues women face, but are too ashamed to speak about. I then told her about what I was currently going through with Storm. She was surprised because no one at work knew anything was wrong, because I showed up every day with a smile on my face, did my work well and went home. But that day, as we stood in the empty parking lot after work, I cried. She didn't judge me; instead she embraced me. She prayed for me, invited me to her church's upcoming women's retreat and gave me the number to join her on a prayer line in the mornings. I cringed when she said 5:30 am, but I did it. The first two weeks, I set my alarm to ensure I was up. Then, I stopped setting my alarm, hoping to sleep a little longer in the morning, but somehow, I would still always wake up and roll over right about 5:25 am! It was just enough time for me to run and pee, then dial into the prayer line. God wanted me to hear something. It had to be, because he definitely woke me up on days I purposely tried to sleep in.

I kept reading and during that chapter, I squared up with the girl in the mirror and the Lord knows, I cried, cried, cried and cried. I was tired of crying, but the tears would just flow. This healing thing was serious; it was deep and painful. I owed it to myself, though. I was on a roll. I was doing better. I was proud of myself. I was making progress on things no one even knew I was dealing with. Therefore, they didn't understand my tears or my praise. I didn't care, though. I just clapped for myself and kept moving.

I also reached out to a life coach and relationship expert whom I met through my travel group. Thank God I hadn't cut all ties from the group as Storm suggested I do. Ron helped me sort through my emotions. He helped me put my feelings and thoughts into perspective. I needed someone who would produce results. I needed a professional, non-bias outlet and he was it. He was tough on me, but I needed it. He held me accountable for my actions, but he also let me know that my grief, pain and hurt were normal. He reminded me that I was human. He encouraged and uplifted me. My emotions made sense to him and my feelings and well-being mattered to him. God knows how much I appreciated him.

I also reached out to a male friend who kept me encouraged by sending me motivational videos and positive quotes every morning. His concern was so sincere. He even offered to go with me to the jazz concert in place of Storm. Although I appreciated the gesture, I couldn't do it. I knew I would've been an emotional mess. It was just too soon after the break up. Besides, my loyalty was still with Storm, and I didn't want him to think I'd moved on.

I was trying to do anything positive and constructive, so the kids and I got together one weekend and created vision boards. I wanted to succeed. I needed a clear visual on the things I wanted. I needed to see my goals, my wants and my needs laid out in plain view.

I started practicing self-love and self-care by spending time alone, by getting massages, pedicures and yoni steams. I was even burning Sage. I even thought about rolling a joint, but I was too afraid of how I would behave while I was high, since I'd never smoked weed before. I just wanted to forget about some things. I wanted to relax my mind and calm my nerves. I wanted to detox every part of me from the inside out, from the top to the bottom. I wanted to get rid of any trace of anything or anyone negative or toxic to me.

I started mentoring a lot more, I even added tutoring to my resume. I also became more active in my community. Those were things that were important to me, but things I had put off so I could focus on my relationship with Storm. I started exercising and eating healthy again.

Although I was getting better, I would have a weak moment where I just couldn't get over how someone who's damn near 50 was still playing mind games. After all, he approached and pursued me, so how in the hell was he not sure about what he wanted? Why did he think it was OK to pop back up in my life, open me up, awaken my love senses and then walk away? Lord, please help me to not just say I forgive him, but to really let it go. I wanted to truly forgive Storm, but not for his sake but for mine, because those damaging thoughts were now hindering my progress.

My pain, anger and hurt would come and go like waves. One day high, one day low, some days it came crashing in and knocked me over. I came to realize that I not only needed to heal my soul, but regain control of my thoughts, which led me to order *Battlefield of the Mind* by Joyce Meyer. I remember reading something about how the fear of the unknown leads to worry, and worry leads to sadness and depression. But they all had to go! Confusion, doubt and anger had to go also.

Then, I asked myself the big question, "Am I the one holding me back?" I wanted the answer to that question, so I ordered *Greater Devotional,* by Pastor Steven Furtick, which is a 40-day experience to ignite God's vision for your life. I felt there had to be a reason for what I was going though. I was not going to let this pain go in vain. This book really opened my eyes and it made me want to figure out what my greater purpose was. As I read through Day 2, then Day 7, I already knew I wasn't living the way God intended me to. As I read through Day 17, I knew I was not walking in my destiny. For the first time in my life, I realized I was just surviving and not living my life to the fullest. It didn't matter that I was one promotion away from making six figures, or that I was renting a luxury apartment while in the process of having my dream home built, or that I owned two nice vehicles and was travelling. I had everything I needed and most of what I wanted, but I was not genuinely happy. The self-evaluation, and the steps I was taking towards healing were doing so much good for me. Lord knows, I was so thankful for those revelations. I needed this to properly move forward. I thanked God for always looking out for me.

> "Every time I look back
> And every time I think back
> On all the stuff I been through
> I prayed through I cried through
> And then I tried you and just when I was about to fall
> Your love caught me when your name I called
> Jesus you keep on looking out for me."
>
> "LOOKIN OUT FOR ME"
> BY KIRK FRANKLIN AND WILLIE NEAL JOHNSON

More time passed and much progress had been made. Kimber and I had the bright idea to reactivate my account on a dating site. I wasn't really ready to start dating again, but we figured it would keep my mind off of

Storm. Keegan's basketball season was over and his grades were back up, the twins were busy with their lives, and Klyde was very busy and excelling in school, so I had a lot of free time and my mind would wander.

Even though I had cut everyone off when I committed to Storm, I still had choices.

It was either the dating site, fall back on that reliable friend, or start fooling around again with the guy I dated before Storm. His name is Tre. But, he was an ex for a reason, right? Tre was waiting for Storm to mess up so he can slide back in. Granted, Tre was very busy because he was a police officer, coached basketball and worked part-time for a travel agency. I love a hardworking man, but Tre was also very inconsistent and full of shit. Plus, I knew I still loved Storm, and I didn't want to use Tre or play with his feelings as Storm had done mine. Then, I honestly thought for a minute that maybe Tre would act right and get it together this time because he knew I'd really leave him, but taking him back also shows him just that, that I'll take him back. It was almost like asking myself, "Do you want to put up with a new man and new pain and heartache, or an old or familiar pain and heartache?" I understood what the singer, Jacquees, meant when he said, "I'd rather be with you and all your bullshit" and honestly, deep down, I didn't want Tre or that reliable friend, or to reactivate my account. I still wanted Storm. Sadly, I was willing to settle for him and his bullshit. I just didn't want to move on or start over.

Wow, the decisions we are faced with can be tough and it's so easy to go back to what's familiar, but I decided against reaching out to Storm, Tre and Mr. Reliable. I went ahead and reactivated my account on the dating site and our bright idea went straight to hell when my first daily match was "Ian Crawford." Kimber and I both yelled "Storm?!" Oh God, the irrational thoughts started again.

Damn, has he moved on already? But he said he couldn't balance a relationship and his career. Was that a lie? Was he on the dating site during our relationship? But, he said he deleted his profile. Wow, I can't believe Storm! Instead of changing his toxic ways, he's just changing women.

What made it even worse was his profile information. It was so full of lies that it made me sick to my stomach. The only thing that was truthful was his comments about his sense of style. He mentioned how he loves to dress nice and that he was looking for a woman who did also.

Honestly, that was when I realized how shallow he was. This was taking me back to a day when he looked over at my Michael Kors purse and said, "You'd look better carrying a Coach." *Huh?* He continued, "You look like a Coach girl." *Well, actually I'm a Ross and Walmart girl.* My mom had bought me the purse for Mother's Day. He then continued to say that he ended a relationship solely because of how "simple" the lady dressed. Why didn't I run then? I was so mad at myself. I think what threw me off was the very next day he came home with a new Coach purse for me. It was always the criticism or insult followed by a gift, or the criticism and compliment in the same sentence.

I took the blinders off and my thoughts became intensified. I started thinking of everything he said or did, like the day we went to brunch and I wore this cute little sundress and some cute sandals showing off my fresh pedicure and polished toes. Storm looked over and said, "That would look better if you wore heels." He always wanted my hair a certain way. He made me feel like I was never enough. I couldn't relax around him. I had to always be perfect and put my best foot forward. Storm wasn't looking for a good woman. He was looking for a woman to look good beside him. Well, if that was the case, why did he question me when I went to the gym? Lord, I was confused all over again. What I do know is that no matter how expensive your taste is, or how nicely you dress, having an ugly personality trumps it all. You have to look good on the inside also.

I was so disappointed in Storm. I was starting to feel angry again. I started thinking, *While I was busy loving him, catering to his needs and wants, accepting him in spite of his past and flaws, I didn't realize he had put restrictions and stipulations on me. While I was busy encouraging, supporting and loving him unconditionally, he had put conditions on his love. I was busy being strong for him, laughing when I wanted to cry or scream, trying to be the best woman I could be to him and in the process, I forgot my worth and what I deserved.*

At that point, I started deleting our pictures from social media. I deleted any post we had been tagged in together. I tossed out anything he left in my car or in my apartment. I threw away any souvenirs from the places we visited together.

Then the questions started. Where's Storm? What happened? I didn't know ya'll broke up! Why? When? At that point, it was hard to say we broke up, because we hadn't. Storm broke me and left.

My stepdad kept saying I was being mean, and I admit that this big heart of mine was becoming cold. I was tired of giving my love, understanding, compassion and effort to people who wouldn't give the same in return. *I always give my all and keep my word. I put myself last and care for others more than myself.* I felt me changing too and hell, who wouldn't? This cold world had won.

My mom was still in disbelief over this as well. She kept saying, "But ya'll were so happy together. I thought ya'll were going to get married. He started calling me mom and he would even stop by here when you weren't here." All I could say was, "I know, Mom." I mean, how was I supposed to act or what was I supposed to say? I was hurt. I was sad. I was clueless. I couldn't explain why I wasn't good enough for a man I'd given my all to.

I then told her about Storm being on the dating site, and that was the first time she lost all sympathy and respect for Storm, realizing he lied about his reasons for wanting to end things with me.

A friend of Storm's reached out to me, and he was feeling the same as my mom. He said he saw the sparkle in Storm's eyes when he talked about me and heard the joy in his voice. He said he was so happy that Storm finally settled down, he also said he thought we were going to get married. All I could say was, "I know."

I ran into a frequent customer of Storm's store and he said he'd been worried about Storm and his behavior lately. I told him we were no longer together. He was surprised, but did say he knew something was going on. So did I, because not only was Storm's behavior changing, so was his circle. He was pushing away the genuine friends that were looking out for him and his best interest.

Then a mutual friend of ours called and said Storm had fired one of the employees from the store. That employee just happened to be that close friend I mentioned before. I'm assuming that's what the customer was referring to, but I had no information to add to that, because in reality, Storm had fired me too.

The questions and comments started to take a toll on me mentally and physically. Yet, in a weird way I felt relieved that everyone else was just as confused as me about Storm. They saw how Storm and I were together. They heard how he talked about us and about our future. I mean, he went from one extreme to the next. One day he was madly in love with me, and the next day, he was just mad. One day he was head over heels about me, and the next he acted like he hated me. I think I stayed longer than I should have because I saw his potential. When things were good between us, they were really good. I kept hoping it would get back to that.

And, of course, as with anything, you have the naysayers. Those were the ones who were waiting for us to fail. The ones who congratulated us to our faces and on our posts, but talked about us behind our backs. The ones who continued to talked about me behind my back.

I will say this, people will quickly get involved with, or form an opinion about, things they know nothing about. But my truth about Storm didn't change just because he's someone's best friend, brother or classmate or because he was a teacher or well-known in the community. The pain he caused me wasn't lessened because he'd never hurt or crossed them, or because he had never betrayed their trust. It didn't matter how much his store was prospering or how good his band was doing. It doesn't matter how long you've known a person, it's much different knowing them in an intimate setting, and I knew Storm all too well.

Nonetheless, all of this was a major setback to my healing. Instead of stepping-stones, I ran into stumbling blocks. I was almost ready to give up. I guess it's true that healing can hurt more than the actual wound, but I had to remember I had come a long way.

CHAPTER 5
WHEN IT RAINS,
IT POURS

It was now almost five months after the break up and I really couldn't understand why I wasn't over him more. I felt that I should have been. I guess I really did love Storm. I was ready to settle down with him. I think deep down I had been hoping he'd get back to being the person he was during the first three months of our relationship.

At this point, I was done with being bitter or angry, but I'd lie if I said I wasn't still hurt and sad. I just wasn't letting it affect me anymore. I was moving forward. Some days, it was in slow motion, but I was moving. I started to smile and laugh without faking it. The crying stopped, and the tears dried up. I realized I could miss Storm, but not want him back in my life.

Maya, Frankie and I were heading to a comedy show one night and we were engaged in our normal girl talk until I opened my big mouth and mentioned that I had seen Storm a few days earlier standing in line at a food truck. I told the girls how I was tempted to call him, but I put the phone down. Maya quickly said, "I'm glad you didn't call and I'm glad you're finally over him!" I laughed and said, "Me too!" But, was I? I was curious to know her reason for the comment, other than she felt I deserved better. I also knew she still wouldn't have minded kicking his ass!

She continued to say she had spoken with one of Storm's exes, and she told her that she and Storm were still seeing each other while we were dating. Even though I had an intuition of just which ex it was, because I had previously heard things about them from more than one person, I tried to act unbothered by sarcastically asking, "Hell, which one, which ex?!"

I really didn't want an answer, so I was glad when Frankie interrupted, until she said "Well, I saw his ass this morning in Walmart with some lady." *What?! Has he really moved on?* My stomach dropped as I asked, "Was she a petite lady?" Frankie looked puzzled, but said she was and asked how I knew. I felt like this information was pouring on me like rain. It felt like I was drowning. I told the girls that Kimber had run into him a couple of weeks ago at the strip club, and he was with some petite lady. Kimber also said that Storm was smelling good as always. I thought to myself, *Yea, smelling like the bottle of Creed I brought him back from Aruba.* Anyhow, I was willing to bet it was the ex that he claimed threatened suicide, and if he had put her through the same shit he put me through, maybe she really did threaten to kill herself. What I do know for sure, it wasn't the same ex that Maya had talked to.

Damn that hurt me bad, but I wasn't surprised. Storm had a reputation of going back and forth between the women he dated and were married to. The ones like my dumb ass that had a soft spot for him and who was willing to let him back in.

I kept my composure as I said, "Well, he seems to be recycling and reusing his women and I'm glad I've taken myself out of the rotation." We all laughed, except I was holding back tears. I was really thinking, *How could he leave me to deal with the damages he caused while he's already in another relationship?*

By that time, we were at our destination. I was ready for some laughs and a good, stiff drink or two.

THROUGH THE STORM

The show was going great, but my mind would wander off, my stomach was in knots. I was hurt, but thankful for what the girls revealed to me. That was my confirmation to move on completely, but my emotions and thoughts took over. *I trusted him with my heart. How dare he take it and crumble it up then throw it back at me and run like a coward.* I was so hot, I thought I saw smoke forming around me. Then I remembered Deuteronomy 32:35 (NKJV):

> "Vengeance is Mine, and recompense;
> Their foot shall slip in due time;
> For the day of their calamity is at hand,
> And the things to come hasten upon them."

His foot will slip, but I wanted to push him!
Then I remembered Romans 12:19 (KJV):

> "Dearly beloved, avenge not yourselves,
> but rather give place unto wrath: for it is written,
> Vengeance is mine; I will repay, saith the Lord."

But that still didn't stop me from wanting to give Storm a piece of my mind. The girls were so deep into the show they didn't realize I had whipped my phone out and started texting Storm. I wanted him to know exactly what I knew and how I felt about it all. Surprisingly he responded right back, but of course, he denied everything, saying that he-said, she-said is childish, even though people saw him with their own eyes. As a matter of fact, he had the nerve to speak to and hug Kimber when they ran into each other. Oh, how I wished that it had been Maya he tried to hug. She would've beat his ass.

But, I wasn't focused on what Storm had done after us. I was upset about him still seeing his ex while we were dating. He continued to say they hadn't been together sexually in over a year. I was thinking, *How old will he be when he realizes that cheating isn't just about sex?* It's the flirting, the lies, the secrecy, the disrespect of conversing with her, the erased messages, the deleted call logs, the meeting up with her when she was in town, the making her feel like she still had a place in his heart. For those of you who don't know, this is cheating.

But his use of the word "childish" stuck with me, because he's not the most mature man I know. Not to mention all the mind games he played and all the lies he told.

What was childish to me was instead of Storm communicating with me, he started deflecting and always made it about him. It was so frustrating because he would never address any issues brought against him, but would instantly bring something else up to change the subject. He would try to downplay my feelings by saying I was overreacting. Yet, there I was being so vulnerable, opening myself up to the beauty and pain of love.

This took me back to a night when I wanted to talk to Storm about his changed behavior, but he waited until I was in the middle of cooking dinner to agree to talk. I politely asked him to wait until I was finished in the kitchen, but he replied, "You better catch me while I care!"

I started to reflect back even further to a conversation during our first relationship. I wanted to talk about the feelings I started to develop for Storm and he replied, "Don't nobody care about how you feel!"

At that point, it was hard to enjoy the show and I wished someone had just unplugged me; my mind was on overload. I was thinking, *So, now he thinks hearsay is childish, but did he think it was childish when he was coming home damn near everyday asking me questions based on what people were saying about me? Or the shit he said his brother thought about me. Was it childish when he called me at work asking me about a meme I posted on social media based on what his cousin interpreted it to mean?*

During our relationship, my social media became such a big issue that I deleted our mutual friends. I deleted people that were friends or family of any of his many exes. I deleted his family, the workers at the store, the band members and their spouses. I blocked people I wasn't even friends with like his ex-wives, their parents and his three sons.

I unfollowed certain petty people and negative pages. I restricted other's access to my page. I didn't care who was offended, because I needed that for my peace.

In one day, I blocked, deleted, unfollowed and restricted over 100 people. There were so many changes to my account that it was suspended for suspicious activity, but there was nothing suspicious about a woman trying to save her relationship. Storm still wasn't satisfied, because the questions continued. I thought everyone was against me, but Storm had me just where he wanted me. I was feeling confused, vulnerable and insecure. I was slowly losing my mind from the hearsay he had incorporated into our daily life. The sad thing about it was now I believed he was just trying to torment me. I believe he was exaggerating about people's responses to my social media page. I mean, why would they care what I posted? Was he even lying about all the women throwing themselves at him or about his exes contacting him?

Sadly, I also later learned that the exact restaurant we sat in, vowing our love to each other the day Storm wanted to post our relationship on social media, was a restaurant that Storm frequented with his first ex-wife.

I knew the girls wouldn't have been too happy with me texting while we are supposed to be having fun at the show, but I couldn't stop. As I debated on my response to his "childish" comment, I started to wonder if men admit it when they're wrong? Do men hold each other accountable for their actions? Do they offer emotional support to each other? Wouldn't it be great if men understood and followed Proverbs 27:17? "As iron sharpens iron, so one man sharpens another." (Berean Study Bible). Real friends don't uphold you when you're wrong.

I remembered how many days I had wanted to reach out to Storm's family because I felt something deep was going on with him, but he had already put in my head that what goes on is his house, stays in his house. I respected him and I cared about his feelings, so I left it alone. Also, I didn't know how he would react if he felt that I betrayed him. Instead, I kept trying to keep him encouraged and uplifted. I just kept praying for him.

Sitting there at the comedy club with the girls, suddenly all the tormenting mind chatter stopped. I sat there, feeling like I was suspended in time, and realized I was as calm as ever. I saw the truth with such clarity that there was no denying it. I didn't lose. I'm a lover, a fighter, a queen, a boss. I am a comforter and a good friend. I support and encourage. I'm a good woman and I know what I bring to the table. I'm irreplaceable, so the loss is never mine. This clarity was not about him; it was about me. I knew Storm didn't get it and probably never would. I decided not to waste my time replying. Storm wasn't ready to acknowledge that his toxic behaviors affected others. He hadn't really changed. Then it dawned on me, the only person I should've deleted was Storm's ass! Off my page and out of my life, and right then, I did just that. I blocked Storm on everything and placed my phone back in my purse and joined in on the laughs with the girls.

After the show, the laughs and girl talk continued over dinner and drinks. Once we were on the road, we laughed and sang. The mood was good, until Maya became quiet. She turned the music down and asked, "Syd, what's *really* going on?" See, Maya was the most empathetic toward my situation with Storm, because she had been through this before. She knew what heartache felt and looked like. I should have known that I couldn't fool her. I sighed. Frankie chimed in from the back seat, "Talk to us, Syd." I felt immediate relief. I began to cry as I prepared to reveal a secret to the girls. Kimber, who was sick and missed the comedy show was the only one who already knew. This was something I hadn't even told my life coach because I knew better. I messed up big time.

Even though Storm and I had ended it five months prior, I was still communicating with him. I had met him for dinner and drinks a couple of times. I was even still sleeping with him, with the last time being less than a month prior.

The car was silent. All you could hear was me trying not to cry any harder. Frankie reached up and rubbed my shoulder and told me to pull over so she could drive. All Maya could say was, "Aww Syd, I'm sorry." But I didn't want sympathy or apologies, because this was all my fault. I fell completely off the wagon. Actually, I jumped off the wagon head-first.

The last few weeks, I had so been hard on myself. I will say that the grief softened me. The heartache and pain made me wiser and the suffering strengthened me. In spite of it all, I was still trying to evolve. I was growing and changing. I was trying to get back to myself.

Maya and Frankie both felt bad for telling me what they knew about Storm, because they knew how much it upset me. But I needed to know the truth, and I knew they told me out of love and concern for me, not to be spiteful. The care they showed for me and my feelings was genuine. Although the information they shared led me down another spiraling hole of darkness and torment about him, this time, I didn't stay down there very long before I came shooting straight up and out of that dark hole and into the glorious light where I could see again.

The old Sydnee was starting to resurface and with all attitude and sass, I thought, *How in the hell did I go from being his girlfriend to being his side chick, or how I went from being cheated on, to being the one he's cheating with? Had our relationship been just a rebound relationship the whole time? Did he use me to get revenge on his ex or to get back at her for something? Did he try to make her jealous with our social media posts? Or did he use me to win her back? How did I go from feeling like the happiest girl in the world, to feeling like the saddest?* Either way it was over. For real this time.

Maya asked how could I even enjoy the show after them telling me what they had. It was hard at first, but I enjoyed being with the girls. They may not have known it, but they gave me strength and hope. Therefore, I continued to hang out with them, even on my rough days. I told Maya, in spite of what I'm going through, I continue to get up and go to church, to work, or to the store. No matter what my current circumstances are, I didn't let that stop me from being on the President's list at school. No matter how I felt mentally, I pushed forward. I refused to let a failed relationship define me, or ruin my hopes of one day finding true love. I was able to enjoy the show the same way I continued to enjoy my life.

I had already let Storm disturb my peace, and it seemed like I was at my "perfect peace" when he showed up wreaking havoc. It was like he waited until I was at the peak of my life to show up and interrupt everything positive I had going for myself. I wasn't going to let him completely destroy the little peace I had left, I wasn't going to let him win, and I damn sure wasn't going to let him steal my joy. I chose to live my life the best way I know how. Happiness is a choice and I had already made myself physically sick by trying to prolong the inevitable.

Through the Storm

It's not easy to detach from people you love and care deeply for, but sometimes it's necessary for your peace and sanity. Besides, love doesn't hurt.

That relationship should have been over. I should have taken those mixed signals as a warning and moved on. Storm's secrets and his confusion about himself messed me all up. Once my energy, spirit and mood began to change around Storm, I should have walked away. His name alone should have been a red flag.

It's like this, no matter what age we are, we're too old to be beating around the bush when it comes to something as serious as a relationship. We need to stop straddling the fence when our actions and decisions affect others. We can't play with people's feelings and emotions because we're unsure about our own. We have to say what we mean, and mean what we say. It's called being honest. Let's all come up higher and walk in truth with each other.

Yes, I had so many reasons to continue to be sad and cry, but I also had plenty more reasons to be strong, laugh and smile.

"Today's a new day, but there is no sunshine
Nothing but clouds, and it's dark in my heart
And it feels like a cold night
Today's a new day, where are my blue skies
Where is the love and the joy that you promised me?
Tell me it's all right
(I'll be honest with you)
I almost gave up, but a power that I can't explain
Fell from heaven like a shower.
(When I think how much better I'm gonna be when this is over)
I smile, even though I hurt, see I smile"

"SMILE" BY KIRK FRANKLIN

I continued to tell Maya and Frankie that shortly after the last night I spent with Storm, I realized things would never be the same. I definitely couldn't love Storm into loving me. I finally accepted what is, rather than dwelling on what was, or staying stuck on what could have been. My peace of mind and health became my main priority and knew I couldn't heal by remaining in that toxic situation.

I then told them about a long message that I had written Storm a few weeks prior. I explained to them, once I hit send, I knew it would be over between us. Storm hates being confronted with the truth, and I spared nothing. Storm hates when I speak up for myself. Storm didn't want to be accountable for my feelings, because he didn't want to be accountable for his own actions. I felt calm even as I wrote it. Not one tear was shed.

The girls were now curious, saying, "Damn Syd, what did you say?" "Was it that deep?"

Hell yeah, it was that deep!! Do I tell them what I said? It was so personal and intimate. Do I let them in on my deepest thoughts and feelings? Oh God. Was I ready to expose myself to the girls?

I briefly thought about it, and decided if I could trust anyone to see me at my lowest and not judge me, it would be these two. They wouldn't ridicule me, they wouldn't judge me or talk behind my back. So, I pulled out my phone, opened it to my messenger and handed it to Maya. She said, "I hope you told his no good ass off!" as she reached down in her purse for her glasses. She was not going to miss a word!

Maya began to read out loud as Frankie listened and continued to drive. I listened from the backseat, sipping on my tea, as if I wasn't the one who wrote it.

CHAPTER 6
I TOLD THE STORM

My Dearest Storm,

I don't even know where to begin, but let me say, this will be the most truthful thing I've ever said to you and the most necessary.

Things happened so fast and I don't know how we ended up here. Just as quick as you forced your love on me, you took it away. I do know that I've been slowly and painfully trying to unlove you. It's happening in small pieces, and it's not an overnight process. It has taken tears, prayers, nights where I couldn't sleep, and days where I couldn't eat. It's not happening as fast as I like, because until recently, I had hopes that we'd end up back together.

I love being in your company, I enjoyed our late night runs to Checker's just for funnel fries, and us eating white cheddar popcorn while watching Greenleaf or NCIS, and that's probably what I'll miss the most, along with your handsome smile and the way you hold me.

I accepted you for exactly who you were. I loved you as you

were. While you were pointing out my flaws, I was merciful to yours.

I poured into you until I was empty. I gave you all of me, emotionally, sexually and physically. There was no hesitation, no in between, no doubts.

I even loved you when you couldn't return the love. Honestly, I think that on most days you didn't even love yourself, making it hard to believe that I did. Still, there I was diminishing myself to prove to you that you were worthy.

I don't know if you put up this wall on purpose, but I tried to love you past your insecurities. I went above and beyond to show you that you were the only one for me and that no other man stood a chance. You already know how I over analyze everything, so if I said I loved you, you should've believed it, because I had already thought of every reason not to.

There would be days where all you would do is complain. You were either so upset with the band members or the store employees that I couldn't even talk about my day. Everything that I was going through seemed so irrelevant because your issues took up all my time and energy. Plenty of days, I left my feelings on the back burner because you were frustrated, stressed or overwhelmed. I catered to you just to bring peace. I bit my tongue. I tried to make you happy, even at the cost of my own happiness, I was OK with that because I cared about you, and in relationships you make sacrifices and compromises. However, I soon realized I was the only one doing so.

On your weak days, I wanted you to still feel like a king, so I would make myself seem weak or passive. I never judged you; I just wanted you to be OK.

I now realize my love isn't for everyone. I see how it can be intimidating to you, because you are content in your pain and you are not ready to heal. I don't regret loving you. I don't regret our time together. If anything, it has shown me what I want and what I don't want in my next relationship. I definitely learned from this, and I will take the lesson with me as I move forward.

I will also say that I never let anyone put anything negative about you in my ear. I never let anyone talk about you to me. I shut down dudes in my inbox. I blocked anyone that could possibly jeopardize our relationship. None of my exes were ever an issue. I was so secure in myself and with our relationship that no one else mattered. I didn't jump at the opportunity when dudes made advances at me. I didn't mind hurting their feelings about you. I proudly told them I have a man. I didn't care what people had to say about you or us, but you did.

You have some toxic people in your life and don't even realize it. Your circle should want to see you doing well, and they don't uphold you when you're wrong. They don't laugh when you fall. They don't watch you spiral down and do or say nothing about it. They help you. They correct you in love and help you move forward. They hold you accountable for your actions, but you already know that, and that's why you've pushed the good people away.

Plenty of nights when you sat on the side of the bed with your face buried in your hands, as I rubbed your back, I would silently pray for you. During your restless nights, when hot tea or melatonin wouldn't work, I would just pray. I cared about you on a whole different level. When you were irritable and moody, that didn't push me away. I wanted to love on you even more.

I waited patiently, hoping things would get better. I waited for you to be the man you said you had become, but you didn't respect me enough to say you were struggling, or to say you had lost interest in me. Yet, you kept me around to stroke your ego, to gain confidence from my affection, from my loyalty and my kindness. You loved the way I loved you, but I'm not mad, because you needed it. You needed me, and the difference with me is that I didn't need you. I wanted you in my life. Yet, there I was exhausted and walking on eggshells around you, because I was afraid you would go over the edge.

There's a void somewhere. There's a wound that needs healing. There's a void in your life that you're trying to fill with women, material things and popularity. You will never find peace or fulfillment in those things until you find yourself. There's a hole in your heart that only God can fill. You need to take the mask off and face yourself. Please stop purposely overwhelming yourself with work so you don't have to deal with yourself. You need to worry less about your outside appearance and work on your inside.

At one point, I was so bitter and resentful during our relationship because I felt that you were taking advantage of my love and feelings and playing on my emotions. I couldn't tell if you were really having a bad day or just saying that so I would go away. I couldn't tell if you really had a toothache or headache like you often claimed, or if you wanted me to just leave you alone. You were never upfront with me. It was a guessing game. It was a daily struggle of questioning myself. Should I let go or fight harder? You wore me out mentally. Through your weakness and insecurities, you made me feel weak and insecure. You strung me along, but I let you. It hurt like hell, but I stayed, allowing you to break me down. Some days it hurt so badly, I felt physical pain. Then you judged me at my weakest moments. You started making excuses instead of effort. Yet, I tried to understand.

Back on your birthday, in awe of how nicely I set things up for you, you said you'd make my birthday so special that I'd cry, and cry I did, but they were tears of sorrow, not joy. You walked away by text and didn't even wish me a happy birthday. I felt stupid. I was hurt and embarrassed. I think the heartbreak was more intense because I trusted you. I loved you, I let you back in and gave you another chance. I fell for your lies again.

The pain was necessary for my growth. I'm much wiser and stronger because of it. You were wrong on so many levels, and yes, so was my reaction. There are some things you just don't do when you know someone has invested their feelings, emotions and time into you, or poured their heart out to you and their love into you. You know there's no halfway with me. Either I overreact or I don't react at all. So, I either seem out of control or passive, but either way, you don't get to tell me how to react to the pain, hurt and heartache you caused me. I feel betrayed and I'm even starting to feel that you used me because your birthday was nearing, and you didn't want to spend it alone like you said you had done the past few years.

Even after all that, we ended up back in bed together, and

the passion was still there and the sex was better than ever. I should've known I couldn't remain friends with you knowing I still loved you. I knew it wasn't going to be easy having casual sex with you, knowing I was still in love with you, but I renounce any ungodly soul ties between us. I renounce any rash vows or verbal commitments we made to each other.

At one point, all I wanted was an acknowledgment of my feelings and an apology, but you couldn't even do that. But how sincere is an apology if you have to ask for it?

I used to pray that someone does you the way you did me, but you couldn't handle that. Now, I pray that you heal. If you don't, you will continue to ruin every woman you come in contact with. I was trying to bring you out of your dark place, but ended up in one myself. I'm thankful for my strong faith, for praying and supportive parents and friends. I thank God I'm strong enough to bounce back, but one day you're going to run into a woman that has no support, and nothing to lose. She's going to either harm you or herself. Will you be able to handle that? You need to know that your actions really do affect people. Please, shift and heal. I pray for you every night, for your mental and physical health. I pray that God will show you your toxic ways as he's shown me mine. I pray he gives you strength to fix them.

What God has planned for me, I don't know. I don't know his plans for you, but I do know we are done. I'm all cried out and there's nothing left for me to say or do. This relationship doesn't need fixing. We both do. I'm tired of messing up and starting over, and that's probably why I tried so hard to hold onto the broken pieces of you.

Through the Storm

I now see that God doesn't need my help. What's meant for me will be mine. I do know that I'm not meant to be lied to, mistreated or disrespected. I'm letting you go. I forgive you.

I just felt the need to let you know exactly what was on my mind and in my heart. I'm tired of holding in my feelings. I think that was a major downfall with us. I was being passive just to keep the peace. Once again, this has been one heck of an emotional roller coaster ride. And once again, I am left trying to piece back my life and my heart after you shattered it. Maybe one day this will all make sense, maybe not. Until then, take care.

Sincerely,
Sydnee

"Even though your winds blow
I want you to know
You cause me no alarm
Cause I'm safe in his arms
Even though your rain falls
I can still make this call
Let there be peace
Now, I can say go away
I command you to move today
Because of faith I have a brand new day
The sun will shine—and I will be okay
That's what I told the storm!
I told the storm to pass

Storm you can't last

Go away—I command you to move today."

"I Told the Storm" by Greg O. Quin

Maya slowly looked up from the phone. She looked back at me with her eyes full of tears. We both looked at Frankie who was now in tears as well. But me, I was all cried out. The car was silent once again until Maya said, "Syd, you wrote that with so much emotion, but kept it classy." Then simultaneously they asked, "Did he respond?!" I laughed because he responded immediately, and he gave the most typical answer that most men give when they've been called out on their bullshit. He replied, "Wow." That's it.

Maya said, "If he had any couth about himself he would've called you, Syd. He would have reached out to you." I laughed and said, "Spell couth." But she was serious and she continued to say, "But he's selfish and he's already proven himself to you." Frankie added, "I can't believe he's never apologized. If he'd just read between the lines, all you wanted was for him to acknowledge that he hurt you, whether unintentionally or not, but he has too much pride, Syd." Frankie was right. Yes, he did hurt me and I wanted an apology.

The girls would be pissed to know that a couple of days after sending Storm the long message, he called me, but it wasn't to apologize. I guess he had time to process what the message entailed, and instead of the apology I expected, he had the audacity to say "your long text almost made me feel bad enough to apologize." I decided to just keep that insult to myself, but that added fuel to my fire. I was more determined to let his sorry ass go. He was burning his bridges and I just hoped he had a boat to save his damn self.

Frankie continued talking, "He knows you're a good woman and he's trying to keep one foot in the door, but you told his ass off and slammed the door on him and his damn foot!" Maya chimed back in, "Yes, you are a good woman and that's why he keeps coming back. Hell, that's why Tre wants to come back, too!" I laughed and said, "That's why they ALL want to come back!"

I love my girls. That night, they encouraged me, inspired me, and lifted me up. They spoke life into me, but I still felt like I was naked. The girls had just got a glimpse of what I'd really been going through and dealing with the last five months. The highs, lows, the good, the bad, the ups and downs. They now understood my emotions and my mood swings and why I was happy one day but sad the next. The journey had been emotional and draining. The girls finally saw what I had been fighting for and fighting against.

Maya said, "What's meant for you will be yours. Stop trying to figure this shit out Syd, he's not worth it." She then quoted Proverbs 3:5–6 (KJV):

"Trust in the Lord with all your heart and lean not unto your own understanding.
In all your ways acknowledge him and he will make your paths straight."

Frankie and I both replied, "Amen."

"If you look at the people in your circle, and you don't get inspired, then you don't have a circle. You have a cage."

NIPSEY HUSSLE

What I had neglected to tell the girls was what prompted me to write that emotional message to Storm, other than "things not being the same." I didn't tell them the real reason I didn't want anything else to do with him.

A few days after our last night together, I had finally gathered enough energy to tell Storm what I had been putting off telling him for a few weeks. I texted him and asked him to meet me at our usual spot downtown. He read the message, but didn't reply. I waited, then I called him. He answered and said he was on the phone with one of his employees and he'd call me back. I waited, but no call back. The next day came and went, but still no call, no text. Late that night, I texted him again, but there was no communication whatsoever from Storm. I hate being ignored. Just tell me if you're busy, in a bad mood, don't want to talk or tell me if you're done with me. But of course, he knew with that, the sex would stop also. I was so hurt all over again, but I knew right then I was done. How could he make passionate love to me, tell me how much he missed me and loved me, tell me I'm his soulmate, tell me how beautiful and sexy I am, beg me not to ever give my love to anyone else, hold and kiss on me all night and then totally ignore me a few days later?

At 3:00 am I began typing that long message. I began pouring my heart out, no editing, no deleting. I said what I said, but I purposely left out the most important part. All I wanted the day before was to tell Storm that I was 12 weeks pregnant. Yes, I was carrying his child, but now I wanted him out of my life for good.

I hadn't told anyone. Not my family, not any of my friends, not even the girls. Storm would have been the first to know, other than my doctor, who was just as shocked as me. I originally went in as a same day appointment because I couldn't keep any food down and I was losing weight. Using the internet, I had worked myself up over the list of diagnoses I came up with, but being that I recently had my annual check-up, as I do every year on my birthday, I could eliminate HIV and cancer off my list. Now, a change in my mental health? Maybe.

But after bloodwork, urinalysis and diagnostic testing, it was discovered that I was pregnant. That, at least, explained why I had been so emotional and crying so much. When I found out, I was nine weeks along and I knew exactly when I had gotten pregnant. It was the week of Christmas. Yes, a little over a month after our breakup. Storm's son was away visiting his mother for the holidays and we took advantage of that. It's like we were making up for that month where we hadn't seen each other. During the nights I spent there, we barely slept. We made passionate love over and over again, and each time seemed to be better than the time before. I'm talking sweat in your eyes, mouth dry, hair pulling, toes curled, body shaking, don't care if you're lying in the wet spot type of love making, and apparently, we were careless. Boy, I tell you that God has a funny way of bringing what's done in the dark to light. This baby was unplanned and very unexpected. Storm didn't want any more kids and neither did I. Klyde was my youngest and already in college. What was I going to do with a baby? Plus, at this point, Storm and I hadn't even discussed us getting back together.

Prior to going to his house that last night, we met for dinner. I thought Storm would figure out I was pregnant because I didn't order an alcohol beverage. He kept asking if I wanted a drink and why I wasn't drinking. I just replied, "I haven't had a drink in about a month." To cut down on the questions, I finally I ordered coconut ciroc with pineapple juice and took one sip. But as soon as Storm went to the bathroom, I had the bartender switch it for straight pineapple juice.

I wanted to tell Storm about the baby then, but I was curious to see how the night would end and where we'd go from there. If we ended up back together, I wanted it to be genuine and sincere, not because he felt obligated because I was carrying his child.

After dinner, Storm was tipsy and horny and all he wanted for dessert was me, and boy was he hungry. I didn't even bother him about wearing a condom and he still didn't catch on. He was just happy to be up in it raw and it showed.

Nonetheless, a week later, after him brushing me off yet again, we were finished. I was done. Him not responding to me when I needed him the most was all the ammunition I needed. I then realized the entire relationship revolved around Storm. I realized the stability of a committed relationship was too much for Storm. With me still sleeping with him after he broke it off with me, I had given him exactly what he wanted—a part-time relationship with full-time benefits.

I had my baby to think about. I won't lie though, I was stressed the hell out. I had raised four kids by myself, but I was afraid of having this baby alone. I was single. I had a full, busy life. I was high risk because of my high blood pressure and because of my age. Speaking of age, I was about to be a forty year old baby momma and Teigan had just found out she was expecting her first child. My child and grandchild would be the same age. I couldn't help but think this is going to be embarrassing and surprising, especially since Kimber was the only one that knew Storm and I were still sleeping together.

I was scared. I had mixed feelings about everything. Do I move away, have my baby and never tell Storm? I've never had an abortion before, but I thought about it for a minute, but then decided maybe I'll keep it. *Yes, I'm going to have my baby. I'll raise it by myself and we'll be just fine.*

Then it happened, again. About a week after I sent the message to Storm, that pregnancy ended the same way my first one did 26 years earlier, on the bathroom floor. For the second time in my life, I had a miscarriage. This time, at least I knew what was happening to me. The pain was the same, the tears were just the same. My emotions were all over. The fact that I had decided to keep the baby didn't matter anymore. Nothing mattered. I was happy I hadn't told anyone. I was glad Storm never knew. I could grieve in private. I could deal with this on my own with no judgment, no questions, no sympathy, no opinions. I wanted to be alone.

I cleaned myself up physically, then I cleaned up what was left of my baby off the floor. I remember how my stomach was cramping as I was on my knees soaking up my baby in a towel—a towel from the Ritz Carlton, where Storm and I had spent his birthday. Then I mopped the bathroom floor. I mopped the guest bathroom. I mopped the kitchen. I couldn't stop cleaning. In the end, everything was spotless, except for me. I was a mental mess.

I stayed in the house for a few days, going from my couch to my bed and back to my couch. I was crying, sleeping, self-medicating. Some days I would overeat, other days I wouldn't eat at all. I was posting on social media as if nothing was wrong, but I'm sure someone sensed the hurt and pain, or maybe I came off as pathetic, bitter and love sick. I had lost so much of myself mentally and physically, and I was hanging on by a thread.

Finally, I got myself together enough to leave the house. I stepped out with a smile on my face as if nothing ever happened, but in reality, the devil was kicking my ass. I wanted to scream, "Lord, help me, please!" There had to be a blessing nearby.

"When I cannot hear the sparrow sing
And I cannot feel the melody.
There's a secret place

Rene Merritt

That's full of grace
There's a blessing in the storm.
When the sickness won't leave my body
And the pain just won't leave my soul,
I get on my knees and say Jesus please
There's a blessing in the storm"

"Blessing in the Storm" by Kirk Franklin

CHAPTER 7
BATTLES AND BLESSINGS, WOUNDS AND WORSHIP

"I think when one discovers himself, he discovers God."

PRINCE

After hearing my message to Storm read out loud, and knowing what I did about the baby, I was determined to be finished with him for good. I know stress caused me to lose the baby and I was tired of the back and forth, the mixed signals and the mind games. Even in all of this, it almost felt like there were still some soul ties between us. There was definitely an undeniable physical and sexual attraction between us.

One day at work, I was talking to a male co-worker, Malone, who happened to have a degree in Psychology. His wife was a psychiatric nurse. I told him how hard it had been to walk away from Storm and our relationship. I continued to tell him how Storm showered me with affection, flattering compliments, gifts, promises for the future, cute text messages, and how Storm told me I was his soulmate, and how Storm and I made love almost every night during the first six weeks of the relationship.

I told Malone that a few months in, Storm started criticizing my every move. He complained about my hair, how I dressed and what I posted on social media, which kept me on high alert. He even complained about me sleeping with my back toward him, when in reality, I was sleeping with my back toward the light and sound of the television which he needed to sleep.

Storm would then give me the silent treatment. Then all of a sudden, he'd start being caring and affectionate again. I described it to Malone as a "nice-mean cycle." I told him how Storm then abruptly ended the relationship.

I told Malone what hurt the most was that Storm helped to pick out the outfit I was going to wear to my birthday dinner, but a week before my birthday, walked away by text.

Malone sighed and said he wished I had spoken to him sooner because Storm's behavior resembled one of his friend's behavior. He said, "Sydnee, looks like you were caught up in a whirlwind of idealization, devaluing, and discarding." I was confused, but Malone continued to explain. "In the beginning of your relationship, Storm love bombed you by overwhelming you with tokens and expressions of love to make you let your guard down and fall in love with him quickly before his mask slipped and his true character was revealed." He continued, "Once he could no longer hide who he really is, Storm knew you were a strong and caring woman who'd fight for him and the relationship. In return that boosted his ego and left you vulnerable." Malone continued, "That's what narcissists do!" Before I could open my mouth to speak, he continued, "By the way, narcissists love to ruin birthdays because celebrations are normally stress triggers, and if you're the target of a narcissist, they hate to see you at the center of attention." Malone added, "Narcissists end things without notice to cause you more trauma and to leave you confused, and in your quest to figure out what went wrong, you begin to chase them, and they get a high from that."

I don't know if I was really chasing Storm, or chasing the feeling he gave me in the beginning.

Our nursing director, whom I had confided in when Storm and I first started dating again, walked up and caught the end of our conversation and said to Malone, "As soon as Storm started to talk about marriage within a couple of months of the relationship, I told Sydnee to run. But because of their history, she thought she was safe." Malone added, "Their history was the main reason she wasn't safe . . . that's called a trauma bond."

Wow!! Trauma bond? Love bombing? Narcissist? Storm? Well, that does explain the gaslighting.

I was speechless. I was shocked. My first response was to laugh, because I couldn't wrap my head around what I had just heard. Mainly because Malone had just laid out my entire relationship with Storm in a fifteen minute conversation. A conversation that made the last ten months of my life come together in a weird way.

At the age of forty, had I been tricked, bamboozled, and finessed? What kind of person had I been dealing with?

Days later, as I was still trying to make sense of my emotions, my feelings and the hold Storm had on me, I ran across a page on social media called, "The Narcissist Exposed" and I began to cry as I read this passage from it:

"When things start going south with the main supply, they pick up the most groomed source and go for it. There is always someone to move from secondary to main, as well as maintaining and acquiring other secondary sources while having a main. And when a new supply isn't groomed enough, they make an ex their main supply again (because trauma bonds are real and the ex is a sure thing) until the new supply is ready. It's a constant cycle and it's a sad way they live their lives."

This took me back to the conversations the girls and I shared on the way to and from the comedy show. The reality was sinking in that maybe I really was just a player in his game. I was the ex that he moved from secondary to main, and once he was done with me he discarded me like trash.

Although I knew Storm was not good for me, I was hormonal, lonely and horny, and I would miss him some days. But I was strong enough not to reach out to him.

Lord, if I fall, let it be forward.

Although I had already started moving on, I wanted to make sure I didn't go backwards, again. I couldn't afford any more setbacks or surprises. As a matter of fact, it had been over a month since our last interaction and that was our text exchange during the comedy show.

I still couldn't figure out why he was on my mind. I just wanted to forget him and the memories we shared. God wants us to have a spirit of power, and a sound mind and I'm thankful that it had been several years since I'd dealt with the spirit of depression, suicide and anxiety. I wasn't where I wanted to be, but I had come a long way. The situation with Storm challenged me. I was at my breaking point. Once Storm realized he was winning, once he realized he was destroying me mentally, I was no longer a challenge and he walked away. That pushed me to the edge, but I didn't jump. I had so many good things going for me. I had so much to live for and so much to be thankful for. I was disappointed in myself and it was hard to understand why I even allowed him to compromise my peace and sanity, my self-worth and my dignity. I worked hard and long on becoming the strong, independent woman I was. Before Storm, I was doing just fine by myself. I was OK with being single. Like Frankie said, I didn't need a king to be a queen. To me, my life was perfect before him, and there I was struggling to get back to that.

One morning I woke up and Ephesians 6:12 (KJV) came to mind. "For we wrestle not against flesh and blood, but against principalities, against powers, against the rulers of the darkness of this world, against spiritual wickedness in high places."

I was thinking, *Whoa! Where did I just hear that verse?* Wait! Oh, my God! I had heard it on the prayer line a few days prior, and as I opened my daily devotion book later that morning, there was Ephesians 6:12 again as the supporting verse.

It was like the Lord was speaking to me and I had learned to take heed.

God was showing me that the devil was after my mind. God was letting me know that the devil was trying to wear me out so he could take me out. The devil wouldn't be fighting me and attacking me this hard if I was on the wrong path. The enemy must have known something I didn't know. Had he peeked into my future and saw the many blessings God had in store for me? The enemy wanted me distracted and that's why he was doing all he could to hurt me, to hinder me. And up to then, he was doing a good job. He had beaten me down. But what he meant for evil, my God meant it for my good. My breakthrough had to be on the other side of this breakdown.

At that point, I was more than eager to bounce back.

"No weapon formed against you shall prosper."

ISAIAH 54:17 (NKJV)

The fact that I was trying to fight against Storm and fight for Storm was helping the enemy destroy me mentally and physically. I was helping him destroy me when I accepted Storm's lies and made excuses for his behavior.

The devil wanted me confused. He wanted me discouraged and weak. He wanted to get in my head and he almost succeeded.

Right then I realized the fight was much deeper than Storm. It was much bigger than Storm and much bigger than I could even imagine. The fight wasn't Sydnee versus Storm, it was Sydnee versus the devil. Once I made that connection, I knew it was a battle I couldn't win alone.

"When there is no enemy within, the enemies outside cannot hurt you."

AFRICAN PROVERB

This wasn't going to be solved with self-love or self-care, or by reading empowerment books. It definitely wasn't going to be solved with pills, alcohol or sex. Many people turn to those for temporary relief or pleasure, but once the high is gone, once you're sober, and once that fun night of sex is over, the pain, hurt and brokenness is still there.

Through this journey, I learned you can lose all the weight you want, get all the massages you want, get eight hours of sleep every night, you can eat healthy, exercise, you can travel the world, or pour a glass of wine with your fancy dinner, you can dress to impress, but if you don't rest your soul in Jesus, you'll never find that perfect peace. Yes, self-love and self-care is very important, and I still enjoy doing all of the above, but that alone equals self-effort. I needed God to intervene.

I knew I needed Jesus and with that being said, so did Storm. It wasn't my responsibility to try and change him. From that day forward, I truly let him go and turned him over to God. What my cousin, Nan, said to me that night finally made complete sense. I was done crying or trying.

Through the Storm

I changed my focus. I needed to equip myself with the full armor of God. I knew He was the only one who could see me through this.

"Ain't nobody stoppin' my shine
They try to break me, try to take me out
But I got Jesus on my side
Felt so bad I thought I would die
But ain't no power stronger than the one
That came and laid down his life
And I got mountains to climb
But the enemy can't stop me
'Cause there's a calling on my life
So, when I'm crying, don't last too long
'Cause he's gon' step in and make it alright
Won't He do it?
He said He would
Fight your battles for you
They gon' wonder how you sleep at night
Won't He do it?
Ah yes, He will
Anybody tell you something different
You know that's a lie
You gon' look back and be so amazed
How it turned out
It's only His grace."

"Won't He Do It" by Koryn Hawthorne

This had been a long, tiresome journey. Lord knows I was getting weak.

"The righteous cry out and the Lord hears them; he delivers them from all their troubles. The Lord is close to the brokenhearted and saves those who are crushed in spirit."

PSALM 34:17–19 (NIV)

God, where are you? I need you. Please talk to me. I'm tired, but I don't want to give up. I know I can't do this by myself. I need you to fight this battle for me. I know I have forsaken you, but please don't give up on me. I just need to feel your presence. I don't want to be lost.

When you begin to trust God, and when you get serious about your faith and spirituality, everything becomes a sign. Everything begins to fall into place. Gospel songs mean so much more to you. Your praise is different. I remember driving in the car, or I'd be at work listening to my music and I would just start praising God or crying. Your praise becomes so personal. Your daily devotional readings touch you in such a powerful way when God is guiding you through something, and the Scriptures start making sense. It's a very overwhelming and humbling experience. Now I am aware that God is speaking to me in everything and everywhere I go. It's hard to explain to a non-believer, or to someone who hasn't met God for themselves.

Even though we went our own way and did our own thing, I thank God that my mom never stopped praying for her children. I'm very thankful she raised us in the church, because the seed was planted back then, and my harvest time had finally arrived.

All of a sudden, I remembered a verse my mom shared with me one day.

"Humble yourselves therefore under the mighty hand of God, that he may exalt you in due time: Casting all your care upon him; for he careth for you."

1 PETER 5:6–7 (KJV)

I cried and prayed, fasted and prayed, prayed and cried. I just needed peace. I needed healing. I needed deliverance. I just needed to hear God's voice.

"Here we are in great anticipation
We have gathered in pursuit of You,
Longing for divine revelation.
Breathe on us with Your Word of truth.
One Word is all we need to destroy captivity
And break the chains that are binding
One Rhema Word designed with your expertise, tailor-made for me.
    Speak Lord, through Your Word reveal yourself to me"

"ONE WORD" BY KURT KARR

I begged and pleaded with God to show himself to me. I tried to reason with Him, but we can't manipulate God. We can't sweet talk Him, but I needed help. I was desperate.

I then remembered Philippians 4:6–7 (NIV):

"Do not be anxious about anything, but in every situation, by prayer and petition, with thanksgiving, present your requests to God. And the peace of God, which transcends all understanding, will guard your hearts and your minds in Christ."

I started praying often. I was praying hard. I prayed specific prayers. When I would wake up in the middle of the night, or when I couldn't fall asleep, I used to cry, but now I started praying and praising God.

One night I woke up around 2:00 am. I had fallen asleep with my music on. I smiled because the song, "He Has His Hands on You" by Marvin Sapp was playing:

"Your days are filled with dark clouds
Even when the sun is out
And from the top of your lungs
You shout, will there ever be a change, what shall I do?
Just know He has His hands on you
He has His hands on you
He says He'll see you through
When you cry, He's holding you
So just lift your hands up high,
For He will provide
Just know He has His hands on you
Sometimes you feel so alone,
Like a child lost with no home
They keep telling you to be strong
But you say, when will it end, when will I win?
But just know He has His hands on you"

I felt a calming spirit come over me. It felt like God had wrapped his loving arms around me. This was much deeper, and way more meaningful than me wrapped up in the arms of Storm. I felt protected. I felt loved.

Over the next few days, everything I learned in church, from my youth until recently, came rushing back to me. Everything I learned from studying his Word, and from the prayer line, were connecting.

I was standing on my own faith. I was depending on my own prayers. "It's me O Lord, standing in the need of prayer." I wasn't relying on my parent's prayers or on my grandmother's prayers anymore. It was Sydnee, kneeling at the throne. I was starting to experience God for myself and what a wonderful experience it was. I started back attending church and paying my tithe faithfully. I was striving to live an intentional life. I knew I couldn't keep sinning and expecting God to bless me. I wanted to be as faithful to God as he was to me.

Everything I knew about my Savior was coming up out of me. God didn't leave me, he didn't forsake me. I was something like the prodigal son, out living my riotous life. Out doing what I wanted, when I wanted. I left God to go out and test the waters on my own, but thankfully, he was patiently waiting for my return. He welcomed me back with open arms.

"We all like sheep have gone astray, each of us has turned to our own way and the Lord has laid on him the iniquity of us all."

ISAIAH 53:6 (KJV)

My mind was racing, but this time it was different and I welcomed it. I needed it. I wanted it. Lord, thank you. I was listening and I could hear him loud and clear. The loud noises in my head were gone, the clutter in my mind had cleared out. I felt free.

Then he laid Isaiah 26:3 (KJV) on my heart.

"Thou wilt keep him in perfect peace, whose mind is stayed on thee."

I was determined to stay prayerful, peaceful and positive.

One night, as I reminisced over my life, I was in awe of God's greatness. I was in awe of his unconditional love, mercy and grace. He's so forgiving, even when we don't deserve it (and we never deserve it). Tears started flowing. I wanted to thank God. I wanted to talk to him. I started asking, "Are you here? Are you near? Please, Lord. Let me touch you."

> "Let me touch You and see if You are real
>
> Even though, I know my heart, Your hands can heal
>
> But sometimes I get discouraged
>
> And I need Your strength and shield. Jesus
>
> Let me touch You and see if You are real
>
> Sometimes to me You seem so far away
>
> And I wonder how to make it through the day
>
> But if I can touch the hem of Your garment
>
> Your power, I know, You can heal. Jesus
>
> Let me touch You and see if You are real"
>
> "LET ME TOUCH YOU" BY KIRK FRANKLIN

I felt his presence. I needed this alone time with God. I had some questions. I went from asking him why to asking him what. What are you trying to teach me God? What do you want me to learn from this? Lord, I need to know, because I never want to feel this way again. I'm tired of messing up. I'm tired of starting over. Please show me, teach me, cleanse me, change me, forgive me. Lord, I'm laying it all on the table.

"If a person does not repent, God will sharpen his sword; he will bend and string his bow."

Psalm 7:12 (NLT)

I started confessing my sins and I asked God for forgiveness.

I continued talking out loud to him. *Lord, teach me patience.*

I am, by placing difficult people in your path.

Is he referring to Storm? Lord, please increase my faith.

I gave you difficult times so you would trust me.

Lord, I need self-control because so many times I let my emotions control me, and during those times, I can't think straight and I become irrational.

None of the fruit of the spirit will develop until something or someone makes you exercise them. Most of the time, it's the wrongdoings of others, and their actions toward you that expose your weaknesses.

OK, so Storm did serve a purpose in my life? I was starting to get it. God wasn't interested in changing my situation, he was using my situation to change me. My God!

Was I being tested? Then I thought back to a book called, *The Power of Praying* by Stormie Omartian. It stated, "There's a big difference between being out of God's will and being pruned or tested by God. Both are uncomfortable, but in one you will have peace no matter how uncomfortable it gets. In the other, you won't."

Then the Lord's prayer came to mind. "Our Father who art in heaven, hallowed be thy name. Thy kingdom come. Thy will be done on earth as it is in heaven." How could I forget that? That was one of the first prayers I learned.

That hit me like a ton of bricks. I wasn't being tested. The problem was I wasn't walking in God's will.

"And be not conformed to this world; but be ye transformed by the renewing of your mind, that ye may prove what is that good, and acceptable, and perfect will of God."

ROMANS 12:2 (KJV)

But God, I prayed for this.

Did you wait for my answer? Were you patient? Did you trust me enough?

But, Storm said he prayed for this also.

I sacrificed, compromised and lowered my standards because I thought Storm was meant for me. I thought he was the husband that God sent, but I was uncomfortable and unhappy. My God is not one of chaos and confusion. I should've known better, but because of pride and lack of discernment, I refused to let go. I let my disappointment turn into despair. I hated change so much that I let a breakup devastate me.

See, the devil also knows what we're praying for. He'll send a lesson in place of that blessing and mess us all up. He knows our weaknesses. He takes notes from our past and learns from our mistakes, even when we don't. That's how he keeps us running around like a puppy chasing its tail. We go in circles; he keeps us in the same toxic cycle. It now seemed like Storm had been preying on me, rather than praying for me. We definitely repeat what we don't repair. He knew to send Storm back my way, and sadly, Storm wasn't the first man I had allowed back in my life after God removed them.

"Teach me knowledge and good judgement, for I trust your commands."

PSALM 119:66 (NIV)

I started praying, "Lord, please help me to recognize who's seasonal and who's for a lifetime. Help me to recognize when someone is having a bad day or in a bad mood, versus when their mask falls off and they start revealing their true character. Help me to know when to let go and when to fight harder. I pray for discernment and I pray that you prepare me for the things I ask you to reveal to me. Help me to stop challenging you. I pray for wisdom, knowledge and understanding."

Storm and I didn't have a connection like I first thought, we had an attachment to each other. A connection gives you power, but an attachment sucks the life and energy right out of you, just as this relationship had done to me.

God had been giving me warning signs, stop signs, and red flags continually, but I drove right past him in the fast lane. I was all in at that point. "Jesus, please take the wheel."

I was making so much progress. That took me back to a night months earlier while I was working on *The Healing Soul of a Woman* study guide. I threw the book across the room; I was not ready to face myself. I didn't want to deal with myself that night. The healing process was taking me places I had purposely forgotten about. Now, I was finally ready.

"Lord, please show me myself so I can move forward and be a better person. I don't want to be bitter. I just want to be better. Lord, please help me to switch those letters."

I know you have a bigger plan for my life and a purpose for my pain. Give me a new perspective on things. Then, I remembered Romans 8:28 (KJV):

"And we know that all things work together for good to those who love God, to those who are called according to his purpose."

111

Purpose? Is this what it means to turn pain into purpose and wounds into wisdom? Then, I ran across Psalm 20:4 (NKJV):

"May He grant you according to your heart's desire and fulfill all your purpose."

Man, that gave me so much motivation and hope. I wanted to turn that pain into power and I was hell-bent on finding my purpose. I then realized that God didn't send a storm to harm me, but to clear my path. God weakened me so his strength could show through me. God broke my heart so his light could shine through. He broke me down to build me up. God bruised me so he could use me.

When I stopped judging myself, I stopped judging others. Then I realized that when we judge others, it's merely a reflection of how we really feel about ourselves. When I started to understand myself, I became more understanding and forgiving to others.

Thank you, Jesus!

Over the next few weeks, I continued to heal. I could feel a change come over me. I was praying, fasting and worshipping. I wasn't just praising God because I needed something, but because he was worthy. I was grateful and thankful. I was feeling blessed.

At this point, I felt like I could relax and stop trying so hard to prove myself to people, and even to God, because I was truly on the right path. Besides that, I was tired. I took myself off the timeframe that society has placed on things like healing, moving on and grieving, because at one point, that was causing me to feel like I was failing. Most people won't talk about their shortcomings or failures. Most won't post their obstacles, doubts and fears. I learned to stop comparing my worst days to people's best days.

THROUGH THE STORM

One morning I woke up, rolled over and looked straight at my vision board. Matthew 11:28 (ESV) stared at me.

"Come to me, all that are heavy laden and I will give you rest."

I rejoiced when I read that. I had worked so hard at becoming a better person and I was exhausted. Thankfully, I finally found my peace in God. I could rest in him. "Lord, here I am!" I needed the rest mentally, emotionally and physically.

> "The spring of April's gone
> The leaves have all turned brown.
> The children are all grown up
> And there's no one around.
> I'm looking over my life
> And all the mistakes, I've made.
> And I'm afraid.
> Somebody told me that You would wash all my sins.
> And cleanse me from the scars
> That are so deep within.
> So I'm calling to You
> If You can hear me
> I don't how.
> I was wonderin' can you hold me now?
> You are the only one that's patient when I fall.
> Your angels come to save me, every time I call.
> You don't laugh at me
> When I make mistakes and cry.

You're not like man

You understand me

See people change

One day, they don't like you

The next they do

I wish that everyone could love me just like You."

"Hold Me" by Kirk Franklin

I started taking my power back from the enemy and from Storm. I was willing to let go and let God have his way. I was wide open. I was paying close attention to God. I whispered, "Lord please show me the way. I'm ready."

"I say a prayer every night, whatever I do, I'll get it right.

With no regret, no guilt or shame this time.

Once I surrender, I won't dare look back, 'cause if I do, I'll get off track.

Move ahead in faith and patiently await your answer, what will it be?

Sight beyond what I see

You know what's best for me.

Prepare my mind, prepare my heart

For whatever comes, I'm gone' be ready"

"I'm Gonna Be Ready" by Yolanda Adams

All of a sudden, I was hearing excerpts from the videos of TD Jakes and Sarah Jake Roberts:

"You mistook that reappointment as disappointment", "you mistook that reassignment as rejection", "he didn't leave you, I removed him", "you prayed

for a good man, but he wasn't the one for you". "That rejection was for your protection."

"Yes, Lord! Keep talking! Please help me to recognize the answer to my own prayers. Help me to let you work this out. Lord, I trust you. Help me to get out of my own way!"

"Hold on and don't give up
Don't you worry.
You don't have to cry
'Cause he, he sees what you're going through.
Yes, he does
God is willing and he is able
This did not catch him by surprise.
So just trust him
And just oh step aside
Be still and don't question it.
These obstacles, they were allowed
He wants to take you higher and higher,
If you will hold on
God is willing and more than able.
This did not catch him by surprise
So just trust him
And just step aside."

"STEP ASIDE" BY YOLANDA ADAMS

At this point, I knew I was going to be just fine. I lost Storm, but I was finding myself. I wasn't where I wanted to be, but I had come a long way. Having a bad day, or a bad month doesn't mean I have a bad life. Having a weak moment doesn't mean I'm a weak person. I can't let what's been done to me dictate my future. I can't let people's opinions of me bother me. I'm a queen, and queens don't beg, we decree and declare.

Everything was coming together for me and slowly starting to make sense. Those cloudy days were gone. My vison was clear. I was completely focused on myself and my life. I was determined to overcome what Storm put me through. My self-respect and confidence had returned with a vengeance!

An out of control storm had passed through unexpectedly. It knocked me over, causing my flame to go out, but when I got up, I rose as the whole fire!

"Shattered
But I'm not broken
Wounded the time will heal.
Heavy
The load the cross I bear
Lonely
The road I trod I dare.
Shaken but here I stand
Weary still I press on
Long are the nights
The tears I cry.
Dark are the days
No sun in the skies
Yet still I rise
Never to give up.
Never to give in

Through the Storm

Against all odds
Yet still I rise
High above the clouds.
Yet times I feel low
Yet still I rise"

"Still I Rise" by Yolanda Adams

CHAPTER 8
WHEN YOUR TEST
BECOMES YOUR
TESTIMONY

"Challenges make you discover things about yourself that you never really knew."

CICELY TYSON

Three months had passed since I lost the baby and let go of Storm for good. Other than seeing him in a commercial for his store, in which I caught a glimpse of his wrist and he was wearing the tiger-eye beads I gave him, I hadn't had any contact with him whatsoever. I think what bothered me about him wearing the beads was that they accompanied a sentimental handwritten message in a greeting card from me. Based on what they meant to me, I felt he no longer deserved to be wearing them.

I hadn't even seen Storm in passing. I didn't care to speak on him and I wished people could have understood that. Storm and I didn't run in the same circle, I didn't hang in the streets much, but I guess since people knew we had dated, they seemed to want to tell me things about him. I didn't care where his band was playing or how his store was doing. I didn't care what school he was subbing at. I definitely didn't care who he was or wasn't dating. Once I wasn't interested in looking back, I knew I was on the right path.

I was so much better mentally and at a peaceful place in my life. I was growing and changing. I was glowing again. I was happy. The most difficult part of the healing process was over.

I wanted everyone I loved and cared for to experience the peace and joy I was starting to have over my life. I wanted them to know how good God was. I started buying devotional books for everyone. Kimber and Frankie were first on my list. Then I got them for all of my kids and their significant others. Next, I bought one for one of my teenage mentees and my youngest brother. My sister-in-law was even interested in reading now as well. For her birthday, I surprised her with *Becoming* and *Healing the Soul of a Woman*. I refused to keep my knowledge to myself.

During this process, I learned that you can't judge another person's relationship with God based on their outside appearance. I was truly changing. Others were starting to notice my change. Some embraced it; others tried to remind me of the old Sydnee. Some friends and family started to act differently and I was OK with that. As long as I didn't lose myself again, I didn't care who walked away.

I always notice things in hindsight, but Frankie and Maya had been telling me about certain people for years now. Although I wasn't all that surprised at some of my friends' behavior, I was still disappointed. That was definitely my year for revealing and removing, and honestly, it was past time for some of them to go. I spent years putting up with the petty comments and sly remarks because of our history. I no longer wanted to be around negative, non-supportive people, and that went for family and close friends alike.

I realized that when you change for the better, some people aren't comfortable with that, because they aren't ready to level up themselves. They prefer to remain stagnant in life and want you to remain stagnant as well. I learned that aging is much different than maturing, growing or evolving, and at the age of forty, I was finally embracing my growth.

Once I confessed my sins and God had forgiven me, there was nothing anyone else could say or do about it.

Once I forgave myself for my past, I started to believe that I deserved better. I deserved more.

I never got involved with that reliable friend again either. We had so much history, but he didn't deserve my loyalty. I think it shocked him once he realized I was really done with him. I was so proud of myself. Frankie and Maya were so happy for me as well. One night during dinner, the girls and I shared a champagne toast to my accomplishment. They knew that in the past he was another toxic person that I should have been walked away from.

I did start back seeing Tre, but that was very short lived. Within a few weeks, I quickly realized he couldn't give me what I truly deserved in a relationship. No matter how hard he tried, consistency and honesty weren't his best traits. I knew I had changed when one night during sex with Tre, I began to cry. I couldn't even fake it anymore. He didn't deserve my body or my intimacy. He didn't deserve my love, he didn't deserve me. At that point, I knew I wasn't ready to explore the dating scene, so I took some time off. Once you realize how powerful sex is, you'll stop giving it up to just anyone. Besides, I wanted my mind and heart ready for the husband that God promised he'd send me. I was done blocking my own blessings. I was ready to enjoy my singleness again. By the way, single doesn't mean lonely or alone.

I was now walking the walk and talking the talk. I had a more positive outlook on life. My life had meaning. I rediscovered my worth and I was on a mission.

A short time later at work, a new director took over and he felt in order for him to utilize every employee effectively, we should all take personality tests. In fact, it was mandated.

What? Is this even ethical? A personality test? What's up with all these personality tests?

As you remember, I had taken one several months earlier during my self-evaluation and soul searching.

Oh well, here we go again.

I logged onto 16personalities.com

As before, I got the letters "ENFJ." I have the protagonist personality: Natural-born leaders, full of passion and charisma. With a natural confidence that begets influence, protagonists take a great deal of pride and joy in guiding others to work together to improve themselves and their community.

The introduction described me perfectly. It also mentioned that President Obama and Oprah Winfrey had the protagonist personality, so I continued reading.

"People are drawn to strong personalities, and protagonists radiate authenticity, concern and altruism."

That statement jumped out at me, and I began to reflect back on something I read on-line after googling "Why narcissists target strong, confident, sensitive women."

Narcissistic men look for someone who can listen to their struggles. * They want someone full of life and positive because draining the energy out of someone already depressed wouldn't be exciting for them. * They thrive on your beauty and diligence and hope to take more power from you upon themselves. * They want to exert power over someone stronger than them. * They want to be in control of sensitive souls. * You make them feel insecure about themselves. * You turn them on with your liveliness, intelligence and lust for adventure; qualities they wish they had in themselves. * They want to make their previous partners jealous. * They want to take advantage of someone smarter, stronger, more capable than them. * They want to steal your inner beauty, because that's what manipulation is all about; tricking a strong sensitive woman into believing she's ugly, unworthy and unlovable.

To read that was very heartbreaking, but it was an eye-opener that made me question if Storm really was jealous of me. It made me think that Frankie was right when she said Storm was intimidated by me. There was now no doubt in my mind that he was trying to make his ex-girlfriend jealous. He used me. Even though it had been several months since Storm and I ended things, this revelation really hurt me deeply. It was hard to believe that Storm targeted me and deliberately hurt me. He tried to destroy me. I can't even begin to describe the pain I felt or the mental anguish Storm caused me. It's crazy, but it felt like the more I tried to love him, the more he despised me.

Reading that also took me back to a day when I was on the way back from one of Keegan's games. As I neared Storm's exit, I called him to see if he was home. He didn't answer the call, instead he texted me that he didn't want to be bothered. I simply replied, "OK." I don't know if it was because I was nonchalant, or didn't give him a negative reaction or what, but a few minutes later he called me to reiterate that he didn't want to be bothered. My response was the same: "OK." We ended the call; and maybe 15 minutes passed before I received a text from him telling me to come over. It was like he wanted to have the upper hand in situations. He always tried to play on my emotions.

That was probably the first time I was able to really grasp what I went through during my relationship with Storm. In spite of my emotions, I continued to read my results of the personality test.

"The interest protagonists have in others is genuine, almost to a fault—when they believe in someone, they can become too involved in the other person's problems, place too much trust in them."

The results were getting more interesting and informative as I read. It was explaining me to me. I was all in. I printed the information out, grabbed it off the printer and continued reading. At that point, it was talking about my strengths. It stated, "Protagonists are tolerant and reliable," and I thought to myself, probably too tolerant. When I got to my weaknesses, my mouth dropped. It stated:

"Protagonists are overly idealistic, too selfless, sensitive. Protagonists have fluctuating self-esteem and define their self-esteem by whether they are able to live up to their ideals, and are always wondering what they could do better. If they fail to meet a goal or to help someone they said they'd help, their self-confidence will undoubtedly plummet and protagonist struggle with making tough decisions, especially when other people's feelings are involved."

Lord, that hit me hard, because it was true. I could've hit the floor. I was 40 years old and just learning so much about myself. How could answering a few questions reveal everything about me? So far, I didn't see any discrepancies.

I was so amazed by what I was reading that Katie was now interested in my results, so I began to read out loud.

"Protagonists take dating and relationships seriously, selecting partners with an eye towards the long haul, rather than the more casual approach, so even in the dating phase, people with the protagonist personality type are ready to show their commitment by taking the time and effort to establish themselves as dependable, trustworthy partners."

My God, the information was so true and deep, that it started to feel overwhelming. The personality test was breaking down things for me in ways I never imagined. I was understanding my "whys" and my "reasons." It was giving me a new perspective on myself, my life and my relationship with Storm. I was finally starting to see how I fell victim to Storm. It also made me reflect on the long message I wrote to Storm.

I kept reading.

"Protagonists don't need much to be happy, just to know that their partner is happy, and for their partner to express that happiness through visible affection. Making others' goals come to fruition is often the chief concern of protagonists, and they will spare no effort in helping their partner to live the dream."

This is where I began to tear up and get emotional.

"If they aren't careful though, protagonists' quest for their partners' satisfaction can leave them neglecting their own needs."

Man, I realized that I let the devil convince me that I was weak and pathetic, when all I really wanted was for Storm to be happy. Yes, I did neglect myself because I cared for him and his well-being and he took advantage of that. I just wanted to take some of the stress of the world off of his shoulders. It was becoming painful to read, but I needed to hear this. I needed this for me to continue getting better. But hold on, because it got deeper as I read on.

"Protagonists' tendency to avoid any kind of conflict, sometimes even sacrificing their own principles to keep the peace, can lead to long-term problems if these efforts never fully resolve the underlying issues that they mask."

That showed me my faults in a lot of situations, not just between Storm and I, but also in my daily life with family and friends. I needed to express myself and stand up for myself in order not to become passive aggressive, bitter or resentful. I needed to stop holding in my feelings. I needed to stop biting my tongue, and this is where I realized that the mental pain of biting your tongue probably hurts more than the physical pain.

I reluctantly kept reading.

"Protagonists invest their emotions wholly in their relationships, and are sometimes so eager to please that it actually undermines the relationship—this can lead to resentment, and even the failure of the relationship. When this happens, protagonists experience strong senses of guilt and betrayal, as they see all their efforts slip away."

Wow, a sense of guilt and betrayal, as they see all their efforts slip away? Is that why I fought so hard for Storm? Is that why I was so hurt and angry?

I thanked God for the information, because it made so much sense to me. I just wanted my relationship with Storm to last, to prosper. I wanted to be his helpmate. Storm was drawn to me for all the wrong reasons. I was literally trying to make it work with him, not knowing his intentions, but this showed me that from now on, I need to learn when to let go and let God.

The devil had taken everything positive about me and made it negative. He took the fact that I had a good, caring heart, a giving spirit and he twisted it up and threw it in my face during my relationship with Storm. The devil used Storm to make my strengths look like weaknesses and there I was being so hard on myself when I should've been patient with myself. I owed myself an apology as well for all the mess I put up with.

Reading the results of the personality test also took me back to another passage I read on "The Narcissist Exposed" page. It stated:

"But paradoxically, empaths will typically block all attempts to have their needs met because deep down they believe that expressing their needs would make them bad, selfish, and defective. And one of the ways they do this is by continuing with the self-sacrificing in the hope that the narcissist is somehow going to turn around and appreciate them for giving so much. So, they are locked in a pathological bind with a narcissist."

As I kept flipping through the results of the personality test, I was overwhelmed at what I was reading, and the reflecting I was doing didn't help. At that point, tears started flowing. It was just too much for me, so I decided I didn't want to read anymore. As I started to fold the paper up, it was like God whispered, *"Keep reading."* So I did, and Katie was still listening with her compassionate ear.

"Protagonists are vulnerable to another snare as well: they have a tremendous capacity for reflecting on and analyzing their own feelings, but if they get too caught up in another person's plight, they can develop a sort of emotional hypochondria, seeing other people's problems in themselves, trying to fix something in themselves that isn't wrong."

Katie stopped me. "Sydnee, didn't I tell you there was nothing wrong with you?!" I replied, "Yes, you did and so did my mom!" Katie continued, "Sometimes you are too much for people and you just have to let them go back to what they're comfortable with. Storm took your good heart for granted." She also said, "Takers only know how to take." That was very deep, because Storm had taken so much from me. But now I had taken it back from him, and then some.

It was hard to see what I was going through while I was still caught up in the midst of it. It was hard to separate fact from fiction, but I was finally at the point where I was done with making excuses for Storm and his behavior. Although I lost all respect and sympathy for him, I continued praying for him.

I finally realized I wasn't broken. I didn't need fixing. I was hurting and I needed healing.

God is so good. It was amazing at how the last year of my life played out. God will give us what we want to show us it's not what we need. He'll show us that our way is not his way. I stepped off his path and took my own, therefore, I learned the hard way. Storm's actions were wrong and hurtful, but I shouldn't have been with him in the first place. People like to say "third time's a charm," but I will stop at two. Storm is a lesson that I will not repeat again.

It's impossible and uncomfortable to try to change who God designed you to be. I was denying the plans God had for me. You can pretend to be someone else and pretend to be happy, but that joy will be temporary. In trying to change who I was for a man that wasn't even assigned to me, according to Joyce Meyer, I was rejecting and disapproving the exact person God intended me to be. I had taken my happy spirit, my good heart and bubbly personality and confined them to the four walls of Storm's bedroom. I was shrinking myself to fit into his box, to fit into his perception of what his woman should be like. I made a huge mistake when I attached my destiny to a person. I settled. Storm and I weren't meant to be. I was meant to be great and to do great things. I was meant to be loved, not just tolerated. I wasn't meant to be used, played with or lied to. I wasn't meant to be taken advantage of. At one point, I felt beat down and defeated. I thought I was losing, but there I was wiser, bolder and stronger.

Strong women aren't just born. We are shaped through the challenges and changes of life. With each challenge and every change, we grow mentally and emotionally. We move forward with our heads held high and with a strength that cannot be denied.

During this journey, I learned that you cannot pour from an empty vessel. We, as women, try to be the perfect mom, wife, girlfriend, sister, friend, employee and we pour into other people and we give until we have nothing left for ourselves. It's past time for us to cater to ourselves. We have to get back to loving ourselves.

I also learned to never measure my worth using someone else's ruler. I am perfect in God's eyes and to the eyes of the one that's meant for me. He will love me just the way I am.

That personality test was truly an eye opener for me and I suggest you take one to get to know yourself better. As a result of reading the results of the test is when I started to believe exactly what Psalm 139:14 (NIV) says, "I am fearfully and wonderfully made!" I was just the person God needed me to be. I was at the exact point in my life where God needed me to be so he could use me. He was building my testimony.

> "So glad I made it, I made it through, in spite of the storm and
>   rain,
> Heartache and pain. still I'm declaring I made it through
> See, I didn't lose, experience lost at a major cost
> But I never lost faith in you
> So if you see me cry it's just a sign
> That I'm still alive, I got some scars, but I'm still alive.
> In spite of calamity, He still has a plan for me
> And it's working for my good and it's building my testimony"
>
> "MY TESTIMONY" BY MARVIN SAPP

Through the Storm

I really didn't lose Storm, because he was never really mine, but I did find my strength and courage. My relationship with God became much stronger. My faith is stronger. God was about to take me places that some people couldn't go. God is the only one who could take credit for what was about to unfold in my life and he was making room for better people. He needed me to depend totally on him, not on man. He needed me to experience some pain in order for him to use me. He needed me to be able to relate to whom he needed me to minister to.

God doesn't make mistakes. We are not here by mistake. You are not reading this by mistake.

Sometimes God calms the storm, sometimes God lets the storm rage and calms his child. If you walk out of your storm the same person that walked in, you missed the lesson. None of us are perfect. Our storms may be different, but we all go through things. Your storm could be your finances, problems in your relationship or marriage, issues on your job or in your church. Your storm could be a troubled child, an addiction to drugs, alcohol or porn. Your storm could be an illness or an addiction to gambling or prostitution.

This time my storm came raging in so confident, smelling like an expensive bottle of Tom Ford, with a chocolate complexion and a perfect beard. He was handsome with a smile that'll brighten any room, and his voice was sexy and deep. His dreads were so neat and flowing down his back. His Rolex was glistening just as bright as the custom rims on his Range Rover. His clothes were tailored to fit him perfectly and not one scuff on his shoes. Lord have mercy. He looked so delicious. I was so blinded by all of that, and so full of myself, that I didn't realize the flooding his rains were causing in my life or how damaging his winds were to my being. When I finally looked around, I was lost. I was caught up in his current,

I was caught up in his web of lies and deceit. Storm purposely rained on my parade and I felt like I was drowning, but thankfully I looked up just in time to see a rainbow. At that moment, I remembered God's promise in Genesis 9:11 (CEV), "I promise every living creature that the earth and those living on it will never again be destroyed by a flood."

God was my anchor and he rescued me. He saved my life. He emptied me, so I could be full of him. God had to make me so uncomfortable, otherwise I wouldn't have moved. God is merciful and his grace is everlasting. Unlike man, his love is unconditional.

I can't help but think back to a song that was played at my dad's funeral.

"It's over now
I feel like I can make it
The storm is over now.
No more cloudy days
They're all gone away.
I feel like I can make it
The storm is over now."

"THE STORM IS OVER" BY KIRK FRANKLIN

I'm a woman who's been through the storm and survived.

When I finally accepted the fact that my perfect way and my perfect timing were not God's, life became so much easier. Instead of needing God to bail me out of situations that I prematurely jumped into, I prayed first, and waited on him before I made any moves. I started to appreciate what I already had, while patiently waiting on what God had planned for me. My focus went from trying to be a good woman for a man to being one to myself. A woman that my children could look up to. A woman that other women could look up to and learn from. My focus went from trying to be loved and accepted to loving and accepting myself.

I was enough. I'm still enough. I will always be enough.

"As for God, His Way is perfect: the word of the Lord is proven; he is a shield to all who trust in Him. For who is God, except the Lord? And who is a rock, except our God? It's God who arms me with strength, and who makes my way perfect."

PSALM 18:30–32 (NKJV)

Fourteen months after I told the Storm, I walked across the stage and graduated with honors, earning my second degree. I started, and was running, a group home for troubled teens. I was still mentoring and had recently won the "Mentor of the Year Award." I was on the board of directors for Nicole's nonprofit organization and I became a member of the local regional chamber. I started dating Mr. Right. Literally. Devin Wright is a youth pastor and supervisor for UPS who came into the group home to personally apologize and deliver some packages that had been previously lost. That day, he was so apologetic, caring and compassionate. He is beautiful inside and out. He's honest. Our efforts and energy match. I can be myself around him. I don't feel I need a full face of makeup on to look beautiful to him. I am not ashamed in between my hair appointments or on my wash days. He's seen me at my most natural state and embraces me unconditionally. He supports and encourages me. He's understanding and forgiving. He loves me on my good days and even more on my bad days. I've never had to ask for his time, affection or attention. We're equally yoked. He protects me. Devin has made me forget my heart was ever broken.

Fourteen months brought on some changes for the girls as well. Maya is now engaged. Frankie is happily married and what a beautiful wedding ceremony it was. I was honored to stand by her side as her maid of honor. Kimber is still single and mingling. Stephanie and her husband are expecting baby number three on my birthday.

Katie has moved on to a much better job that is closer to her home. I miss her a lot. I'm not sure if she knows how much she meant to me. I appreciated her wisdom, her prayers, her honesty and her knowledge. Katie kept me grounded.

If not before, I truly believe in fate and destiny now. I truly believe that life makes a full circle and we reap what we sow. We need to start applying the golden rule to our lives. We get what we give. If we want better, we have to do and be better as a person. If we want good friends, we have to stop and ask ourselves are we even friendly? Are we honest, reliable and loyal? Are we dedicated and committed to being the good spouse that we're looking for?

I said that to say the coworker that prayed for me and invited me on the prayer line ran into hardships of her own. I was able to be there for her spiritually, mentally and physically without judgment. That's what women are supposed to do for each other. I took her under my wing and sheltered her from the storm she was going through, just as she did me. God works in mysterious ways. He places people in our lives for a reason, just as he removes them for a reason.

As far as the kids, Raigan's marriage is back on track. She and her husband are expecting a baby boy at anytime.

Teigan is doing well. She and her husband were blessed two times over with twin girls.

Keegan graduated from college and is now in grad school working on his master's degree. He recently proposed to his girlfriend and she accepted.

Klyde is going into his senior of college and already working in his field.

Eventually, I ran into Storm and we finally talked. He gave me such a sincere apology that it almost brought tears to my eyes. He told me he was in counseling and it showed. His demeanor was different, his tone was different. His eyes were no longer empty. He asked for my forgiveness, but little did he know I had already forgiven him.

Storm was doing well for himself and honestly, I was happy to see that, because I never stopped praying for him. He had completely retired from teaching, and was now mentoring and coaching wrestling. His business and band were both doing great. Storm was recently featured as the "Hometown Hero" in one of our local newspapers, in which I voted for him.

Seeing Storm took me back to a dream he shared with me one morning as we lay in bed. He told me he dreamt that we were both doing amazing things for our community and that we were both making a difference in the lives of our youth. He said, "Syd, God revealed to me that we're going to be a powerful force in our community." I laughed and said, "Yes, we'll be a power couple." As Storm rolled over to kiss me, he agreed, "Yes Syd, we're going to be a power couple."

What's amazing is that Storm's dream came true. We were both doing amazing things for our community and for our youth, but just not as a couple. Storm's dream came to life, but not how we expected it to, but just as God intended it to.

Life is great and there is no denying that God is good.

"Now every time I witness a strong person, I want to know: what dark did you conquer in your story? Mountains do not rise without earthquakes."

KATHERINE MACKENNETT

CONCLUSION

I hope you enjoyed reading Sydnee's story as much as I enjoyed writing it. I'm no life expert, but just like in the work industry, sometimes experience trumps a degree. My own experiences and the experiences of the many women in my life is what I used to guide me as I wrote this book.

Much like myself, Sydnee isn't a simple woman, but rather a complicated mixture of pain, love, loss, faith, broken pieces, perseverance, mistakes, grace, disappointments, prayers, and a major comeback.

And, just like Sydnee, Storm isn't just an individual, but a mixture of flesh and spirit. He's a blend of hurt, bad choices, failed relationships, ugly truths, life lessons, secrets, and stumbling blocks.

The definition of a storm is "a disturbance of the normal condition of the atmosphere, manifesting itself by winds of unusual force or direction, often accompanied by rain, snow, hail, thunder, and lightning, or flying sand or dust."

This sounds a lot like the Storm that made its way through Sydnee's life.

Sydnee experienced a lot of stormy and challenging days, but kept quiet about them. She didn't tell her family and even what she told her friends was always filtered and softened. She realized she kept quiet because she was embarrassed. She also thought she would be labeled as the 'bad guy' for speaking up or speaking out. She then started to chase the sunny, good days, and even welcomed the overcast days where things were just tolerable and ordinary with no major disturbances.

Domestic violence can be so easy for other people to ignore because it often happens without any witnesses and it is sometimes easier not to get involved. Also, with emotional and psychological abuse, there is no physical evidence—no scars, marks or bruises.

Another part of why domestic violence is allowed to continue is because there is often an unwritten rule in many families: Don't ask. Don't tell. Yet, speaking out against domestic violence can change attitudes towards violence, whether it is physical, sexual, emotional or psychological.

Sydnee had no idea of the type of relationship she was in until she was out of it and on her road to recovery. Like most women, Sydnee didn't know until much, much later that the first step in most domestic violence relationships is to seduce, charm and love bomb the victim. Had she known, had she not ignored the red flags, had she confided in her friends or a professional sooner, perhaps she wouldn't have stuck around for the next step of Storm trying to isolate her from family or friends or devalue her by putting her down continually. The abuser may also take away his emotional or physical intimacy, take way his affection, or he will purposely slow down his contact with the victim.

Although we need the stormy, rainy days and the overcast days to help us appreciate the sunny days, we must recognize when the bad far outweighs the good. It is critical to recognize when it's time to seek help or run for shelter. Storms are beneficial to us only if they help us to grow and learn.

I personally liked Sydnee's resilience. I liked her determination to evolve and grow, no matter what obstacles or challenges she faced. Each time she fell, she got up stronger, wiser and bolder.

I enjoyed seeing her turn her lessons into blessings, her pain into power and her wounds into wisdom.

If I could take anything from Sydnee and apply it to my daily life, it would be her faith, her courage, her strength, and the unconditional love she gave.

There is power in storytelling and, in that, healing. Let's commit to no longer being manipulated or controlled by hurt, guilt or shame. I pray that in one way or another this story has inspired you, encouraged you, empowered or motivated you. I pray that you never lose your voice, and that you not only own your truth, but always speak your truth.

Blessings,
Rene N. Merritt

Thanks for the love & support!

Love,

Rene

FROM MARRIAGE.COM /ADVICE/DOMESTIC -VIOLENCE-AND-ABUSE

"Abuse is a complex concept, one that is easily defined and yet very difficult to understand and identify. Many who have experienced abuse in any form for long periods of time or from a number of people in their lives have difficulty distinguishing unhealthy relationship patterns and the dangers of prolonged abuse. The term "abuse" covers a broad spectrum of behaviors and actions thus making it difficult to define a specific number of types. The following examples are the most commonly recognized types of abuse in a partnership, marriage, or long-term relationship."

Emotional abuse is perhaps one of the vaguest types of abuse to which an individual can be exposed. Emotional pain and hurt are not uncommon in relationships—it is human to feel negative emotions in response to arguments or unpleasant events in a relationship. While it is natural to feel emotional responses, it is not healthy or natural to feel as if your thoughts, feelings, and emotions are regularly threatened by your loved one. Emotional abuse is a consistent denial of your right to express your feelings. It is a violation or ridicule of your most important values and beliefs. Some warning signs that you may be experiencing this type of abuse are:

- Withholding of approval or support as a form of punishment,
- Criticism, belittling, name-calling, and yelling,

- Regular threats to leave or being told to leave,
- Invasions of privacy, and
- Elimination of support by preventing contact with friends and family.

Psychological abuse is also difficult to define as it encompasses a spectrum of abuse that offers no obvious physical evidence. Psychological abuse can be included as an element of emotional or verbal abuse, making it difficult to define it as a distinctly different form. Many experience this kind of abuse in the form of restriction, belittlement, unrealistic demands, or threats. It can also include things such as withholding affection/information in order to extract certain behavior from the individual being abused. Many of the signs of this type of abuse are similar to those of emotional abuse. Examples include:

- Refusal to socialize with the victim,
- Taking car or house keys from the victim to prevent escape or safety,
- Threatening to take the children,
- Playing mind games, and
- Ignoring or minimizing the victim's feelings.

These are only two forms of identified abuses. If you are concerned for yourself or someone you love, get more information. Go to thehotline.org. Don't wait another day to get help.